CW00687807

Sexy Surprises with an Ex

Sexy Surprises, Volume 22

Giselle Renarde

Published by Giselle Renarde, 2023.

Sexy Surprises with an Ex © 2023 by Giselle Renarde

All rights reserved under the International and Pan-American Copyright Conventions. No part of this book may be reproduced or transmitted in any form or by any means, electronic or mechanical, including photocopying, recording, or by any information storage and retrieval system, without permission in writing from the publisher.

This is a work of fiction. Names, places, characters and incidents are either the product of the author's imagination or are used fictitiously, and any resemblance to any actual persons, living or dead, organizations, events or locales is entirely coincidental. All sexually active characters in this work are 18 years of age or older.

This book is for sale to ADULT AUDIENCES ONLY. It contains substantial sexually explicit scenes and graphic language which may be considered offensive by some readers. Please store your files where they cannot be accessed by minors.

Cover design © 2023 Giselle Renarde

First Edition © 2023 Giselle Renarde

All stories in this collection have been previously published.

Warning: the unauthorized reproduction or distribution of this copyrighted work is illegal. Criminal copyright infringement, including infringement without monetary gain, is investigated by the FBI and is punishable by up to 5 years in prison and a fine of $250,000.

Table of Contents

Sexy Surprises | with an Ex 1

Current and Former Loves 2

Pussy Breath 12

Secret Mercy 17

Capture the Bride | 1 27

2 32

3 36

4 41

5 46

6 50

7 53

8 59

9 63

10 68

11 74

12 79

Spite Sex 85

Running in Circles 89

You might also enjoy: 99

ABOUT THE AUTHOR 101

Sexy Surprises
with an Ex

6 Erotic Stories
Giselle Renarde

Current and Former Loves

He's never going to give up, is he?

You'd think that, after seven years apart, he'd have moved on and found someone else. It's kind of pathetic that Red still sends you those mushy greeting cards, professing his undying love. Pathetic, and also a little heartrending.

Nate isn't threatened. Of course he's not. Nate's not threatened by anything. Red knows you've moved on—you told him three years ago that you're with someone else. He makes fun of Nate's name, which used to piss you off, but now you think it's kind of funny. Nate is the first person to poke fun at himself.

"Let's have coffee," Red writes in a Valentine's Day card. "We can catch up. It's been forever. I miss you."

You consult Nate. He isn't much help. You want him to fly off the handle, get all jealous, forbid you from seeing your ex, but he only says, "Do whatever you feel is best."

"I don't know what's best," you tell him. "Red can be pretty persuasive. I can't even convince him to stop sending these stupid cards."

You say they're stupid, but actually they're kind of sweet. Nate never gives you cards.

When you get Red on the phone, you regret calling. Just hearing his voice after all these years makes your heart ache.

Worse yet, his familiar tenor summons a throb between your thighs. Why are you so turned on by your ex? Well, that's a stupid question. He was always incredible in bed.

"Coffee," you tell him, feeling utterly inarticulate. "We could... go?"

"Actually, I'm free for dinner."

"Dinner?" I ask, looking to Nate for answers.

"I could take you to that place you like, with the thin-crust pizza."

"No, that place shut down."

"Oh."

"Invite him here," Nate whispers. "I'll cook."

You can't imagine how that would go down, but the invitation flies out of your mouth before you can catch it. And Red agrees. He says, "It'll be good to meet the man who replaced me."

What the hell? You shake your head, close your eyes, but this thing is happening whether you like it or not.

Nate goes all out—the full meat and potatoes experience. He's so casual about it, not threatened in the least. Does he not understand how much Red still wants you?

The phone rings, and your stomach drops. You know it must be Red. Your hands are shaking as you buzz him in.

"He's coming," you tell Nate, who is busy steaming peas. "He's coming up. Right now. How do I look?"

Nate shoots you a knowing glance. "How do you want to look?"

"Ugh! You're no help." You rush to the bedroom to check yourself in the mirror. Is this blouse too low-cut? Will it give Red the wrong impression? You look amazing. Too amazing.

There's a knock at the door, and Nate gets there first. You watch from the wings as Red hands him a bottle of wine. There's nothing strained about their meeting. Nate welcomes Red into your home. Of course, Red's been here before. He's sat on that couch. He's slept in that bed. He's been all over.

None of that seems relevant to Nate.

When you finally step forward, the air is electric. Red looks you up and down and you're afraid your knees are going to buckle. The way he gazes at you, so fiery and forceful, makes you want to bend over right now.

Nate goes back to the kitchen. You don't know what you talk about with Red. You lead him inside. He opens the wine. You're talking about something, making pleasantries, but you can't even hear yourself. Your brain is caught in a feedback loop.

Dinner goes by the same way, with lots of talking and laughter. Nate is so comfortable. Red sits up straight and chews his meat, but you're off in another world. This doesn't seem real.

Over dessert, Nate says to Red, "Look, it's obvious there's still something between you two. Why not get it out of your systems?"

You drop your spoon in the butterscotch ripple. "Nate!"

"He's right," Red says.

You wait for an argument to break out, or for something to happen, but the men just look at you, expectantly. How the hell are you supposed to respond?

Red finishes his ice cream. "You look incredible tonight. Good enough to eat."

"Oh."

Nate starts clearing the table. He says, "Why don't you two head into the bedroom? I'll be right there."

"What?" You can't help feeling like the pawn in some scheme of theirs. Are your current and former boyfriends in cahoots? "You want... right now?"

"No time like the present." Red stands and your eyes are drawn directly to his crotch. God, is he hard! You can see the outline of his erection through his pants. You'd almost forgotten how huge he is.

Your legs wobble, and it has nothing to do with the drink. Red escorts you to the bedroom. He actually takes you by the arm and walks you there. Nate watches, smiling gently. This can't be happening.

Red closes the door, then pins you against it, kissing you so hard your knees give out. What's happening? Your tongue responds and your feet find the floor. Your strength returns. In fact, you feel super-human as you push against Red's body. He isn't going anywhere. He's got your arms and he's holding them tight, but you're straddling his thigh. Your hot pussy moves against him, gently at first, but it's enough to coat your panties with a slick layer of juice.

"God, I've missed you," Red growls.

"Me too," you say, but it comes out like a squeak.

When you look into his eyes, you see your past. You feel every fuck he's given you—every ruthless, jarring, insatiable fuck. And you want it again. You grab his cock.

"Oh, you little slut." He shakes his head, sneers. "You little fucking cock-slut!"

You whimper when his hot lips land on your neck. He kisses that sensitive spot, tickling you with his muzzle, but you don't laugh. This isn't funny. You moan, haunting your own bedroom.

How could he still be this hung up on you after so many years apart? Isn't it pathetic that he hasn't found someone else? Or is it sweet? He's been pining over you. He's imagined this moment for seven years, and here you are, kissing him, craving him, while Nate...

"Can I come in?" Nate asks through the door.

Your heart clenches. Why do you feel so guilty? This was his idea. He won't be mad.

Red pulls you to his chest and you feel the door open against your back. When Nate slips into the bedroom, your skin prickles. You're trapped in Red's arms, breathing hard as your breasts swell against his front.

Nate asks, "What are you waiting for?"

"I don't know." Your heart races. Your pussy throbs. "Aren't you... Isn't this weird?"

Nate makes his way across the room, taking a seat in the reading chair. "Red wants you. You want him. It's not like you've never done this before."

True enough. When you and Red were a couple, you fucked like rabbits. Red was so forceful, so secure. He would grab you, corner you, do you in public, whenever the mood struck. He couldn't get enough, and you loved that about him.

Hard to believe, all these years later, he still wants you. He's like a teenager—a strapping, muscular, horny teen.

"Take off her clothes," Nate says, like he's calling requests to a lounge lizard. "Bend her over and give it to her, Red."

You can hardly believe your ears. What's the opposite of jealousy? Because Nate's got a raging case of it.

Red doesn't ask questions. He's like a sexy automaton doing the bidding of Master Nate. While Red untucks your blouse, you work at the buttons. If Red gets his hands on them, they'll probably go flying across the room.

He slips the satin fabric down your shoulders, and you feel naked already. A growl rises in Red's throat as he watches your breasts heave inside your bra. He pushes your tits together until your nipples pop out of the cups. He doesn't waste a second before diving at your chest.

His mouth finds a pebbled pink bud and sucks so hard you shriek.

Nate gasps from across the room.

You look at him because you're sure he must be mad. But he's not. Oh no. His eyes glaze, but he's smiling. He's also rubbing his cock languorously through his pants.

"Red, that hurts," you say, pushing his large shoulders. "Gentle, please."

"He doesn't do gentle," Nate says.

"That's right." Red dives at your other breast, but it doesn't hurt this time. He's taking notes, even if he won't admit it. His mouth is hot and mean, nothing like Nate's. Actually, Nate is better with his mouth than Red ever was. Rough is good for fucking. Licking is a whole different ballgame.

"Fuck me," you moan. "God, I need it."

Is that insulting, to Nate? He doesn't seem to notice. His fist is wrapped around his thick shaft, pants and all. He's stroking it good and slow. Your mouth waters. You want to suck his cock, but how the hell would that work?

Doesn't matter. It's not going to happen. Red flips you over so your tender tits pang against the mattress. He tosses up your skirt and kneads your exposed ass cheeks. You don't often wear thongs, but you used to, back when you and Red were together. It's a blast from the past.

"I love your ass," he says, dropping his pants and resting his hard cock in your crack.

You moan uncontrollably. You can't find words, but you don't need them. You don't need to be articulate to get fucked.

Nate says, "I love those dimples she has, right at the top."

Red flips your skirt up even higher. "Yeah, those are great."

"I love the way her asshole puckers, like it's got something to hide."

"Oh yeah." Red tears off your thong and pushes your cheeks apart. "Look at that—it's winking at me."

They're talking about you like you're not in the room, and you don't even care. You just want to get fucked. Nothing else matters. Doesn't even matter that your partner and your ex are staring at your asshole. As long as Red doesn't try shoving his massive dick in there, everything's cool.

Your pussy's so wet that juice is leaking down your thighs. You're slick and ready, throbbing for cock. The men are watching your asshole clench, laughing at you, but you don't give a fuck. Your pussy is swollen and hot, and they've got what you need.

"Fuck me," you growl. You're an animal, clawing at the bedspread. "Fuck me *now*!"

When they both stop laughing, their silence is stifling. It hovers over the room like a dense fog.

"Fuck her," Nate says, quietly. Barely a whisper. "Go ahead. Fuck her."

Red swallows hard. The heat of his naked crotch bakes your butt. You thought nothing could be hotter than your pussy, but when his cockhead meets your swollen slit, it's hotter than hell.

"Push it in," Nate says. "Sink right into her, balls-deep."

"Yeaaah!" Red groans as he drives into your wet cunt. It pangs when he bottoms out. You shriek, but he doesn't let up.

"Again," Nate begs. He might even want it more than you do. "Fuck that slut, Red."

You gasp because Nate has never called you a slut. You wanted him to, in the beginning, because Red used to slut-shame you and you loved it. But Nate wouldn't do that. Never.

"Look how wet she is," Nate says. He sounds closer now. "Her pussy juice is all over your dick."

Red groans and you wonder... did Nate just touch him? A warm, wet finger prods your asshole, and your fuzzy brain puts two and two together: Nate stroked the base of Red's cock to steal some pussy juice. Even if that's not really how it happened, you like the image. And you love that finger poking your hole. It builds the pressure of Red's cock ramming you.

You'd forgotten it was possible to come like this. Alone or with Nate, you need a ton of clit stimulation. Red can fuck you into a frenzy. His dick will get you there. He pounds your pussy while Nate fingers your ass. You can feel your cheeks jiggling every time his pelvis smacks them.

"Yes!" you scream. "Yes! More!"

His huge cock reams you. Was it always this thick, or have the years apart fostered growth? Maybe Red's dick has been swelling with grief since the day you broke up.

Red growls as he bangs you. He's an animal, digging his filthy paws into your ass cheeks while Nate works at your hole. Together, they're getting you there, and fast. You can't believe how hard Red's going at you. His balls smack your pussy while his cock fills you. He packs that dick in like nobody's business. He makes you pant, makes you moan.

When Nate says, "Come," you're ready.

"I love your fucking cock!" you cry, throwing yourself back into the saddle of Red's hips. "God, it feels good."

"God, it *looks* good!" Nate fucks your ass with his finger.

How is there enough space in you for all that? You're packed. You're full. Every time Red pounds you, you feel it in your toes. You feel it in your tits. You feel it everywhere.

You're screaming. The sounds streaming from your lips aren't real words, just strings of cuss-like syllables. Your brain has flown the coop. You're all body now—all lust and blush and orgasm. Red could always get you there.

When Nate pulls his finger out of your ass and Red pulls his cock out of your pussy, you're barely conscious. A torrent of cum spills across your backside. That wakes you up. Your pussy's still ringing as cream streaks your skin. It's hot and sticky.

God, that feels good.

Your heart beats in your throat. Nate and Red are talking, laughing, but you can't make out a single word. You're bent over the bed, panting so hard your lungs hurt. Your body is spent and sore, but you feel energized. Maybe not energized enough to stand or move, but energized.

God only knows how much time has gone by when Nate jostles you. "Red's leaving now."

In your bra and your skirt, you hobble to the door and say your goodbyes to bright-eyed Red. You've never seen him so happy. He kisses your cheeks and says, "See you soon."

"Soon...?"

You're dazed and confused. When Red is gone, you look to Nate for answers.

"We haven't seen the last of that guy," Nate says. "Once a week—all three of us. Is that too much?"

This can't be real. Did Nate really set up a standing date with your ex? That's crazy. What is with these guys? They must be the least jealous men on the planet. It's like all they care about it your happiness, your pleasure... *you*.

You're not sure how to respond, but it turns out you don't need to. Nate pins you against the front door. No escape. His hard cock pulses against your belly, igniting your desire. "Got room for one more?"

Pussy Breath

Odessa tried hard to sniff her pits without alerting the receptionist. New client meetings were nerve-wracking enough without the added stress of pitting out a satin blouse before nine in the morning.

She tried to convince herself there was nothing more empowering than walking into an important business meeting with the scent of pussy on her breath.

Somehow, she remained unconvinced.

Would her new client approve of hooking up with an ex before work?

Odessa couldn't say what had come over her. She wasn't normally like this. To her credit, she'd planned to be forty minutes early. That's how she knew she had time to pop up and see Jalisa.

This hook-up was entirely unplanned. Entirely.

Well, not *entirely*.

When she'd mapped her route, she noticed the client's office was dangerously close to Jalisa's condo building: down the street, around the corner, then along the way just a couple blocks.

Dangerously close.

Still, Odessa didn't plan to leave extra early so she'd have time to show up on Jalisa's doorstep. She just happened to wake at an ungodly hour and leave the house with plenty of time to spare. These things happened.

She arrived in the vicinity far too early. What choice did she have but to visit Jalisa?

Jalisa opened the door wearing dark grey yoga pants and a turquoise sports bra. That shade of blue really popped against her golden-brown skin. She flicked her black ponytail behind her shoulder and said, "Took you long enough."

Odessa didn't know how to respond. They'd broken up three years ago. She figured her ex would have moved on in a heartbeat. Jalisa was such a catch: fit and fun and drop-dead gorgeous.

Jalisa turned away from the door. She walked across the small living space, where a fitness routine played on the television screen. When she hit the yoga mat, she stripped off her sports bra.

Odessa quickly closed the door so the neighbours wouldn't see.

Jalisa pushed down her yoga pants, bending low enough that Odessa caught sight not only of her sculpted ass, but her large breasts as well.

A peek was more than enough to get Odessa pulsing with anticipation.

Naked, Jalisa made her way to the sturdy granite countertop that served as an eating nook. She hopped up, spread her legs, and beckoned Odessa to eat.

Odessa sped toward her ex, climbing gracelessly onto the nearest barstool. She hadn't removed a strip of clothing.

Jalisa raised those legs in the air, leaned her elbows back, and steadied her feet against the counter.

Odessa knew she was merely there to serve.

She planted her face in her ex's pussy and inhaled deeply. She could smell sleep and the start of an exercise routine. The aroma made her wild inside, and the soundtrack from whatever fitness program was on TV didn't hurt. The music had a rapid pace and thumping bass, which suited the moment.

Odessa inched her lips closer to Jalisa's shaved pussy and fought the urge to wrap her mouth around those gleaming lips, bite down hard, gnaw and tug.

Jalisa's pussy looked perfectly presentable.

A knot developed in Odessa's stomach when she wondered who that was for.

Silly question. Jalisa kept her pussy shaved because that's how she liked it. She felt comfortable that way. It wasn't for anyone but her. Jalisa acted only for Jalisa. She was her own greatest advocate and representative.

Enough thinking. No time. *You're on the clock, Odessa. You've got a meeting to get to. Just eat this pussy and get the hell out!*

Jalisa sped things along by cupping the back of Odessa's head and pressing her face into that sweet pussy.

Odessa couldn't complain. There's nowhere else she'd rather be. She circled her lips slowly around Jalisa's clit, then picked up speed, expanding the loop. Jalisa liked that, oh yes. She groaned like she hadn't been touched in many months.

Possibly years.

But that was impossible. A beautiful woman like Jalisa? She'd be fending them off with a stick. She could have anyone.

Odessa opened her mouth as wide as she could and sucked every inch of pussy inside. Not just Jalisa's clit and inner lips, but the outer ones, too. She sucked in pulses. This was the most efficient way to make Jalisa come. Her ex wasn't one for licking. When you went down on Jalisa, you had to make a statement.

This was Odessa's statement: *I can vacuum your pussy between my lips. I create suction like no one else.*

Did you miss me?

Jalisa dropped both feet on Odessa's shoulders and leaned back, so she was lying flat on the granite, with her head falling into the empty sink. You had to utilize every bit of space in a small condo. Odessa remembered having sex in every corner of every room.

They'd done it everywhere, all over, when Jalisa first moved in.

She sucked ardently at her ex's pussy, making Jalisa squeal and moan. That's all it took. Just keep sucking. Doesn't take long to make Jalisa come.

Odessa didn't stop just because her ex hit a climax. She kept at that sweet pussy, sucking down its fluids, enjoying the hold she had over Jalisa in that moment. It wasn't often she felt in control, but when she wrapped her mouth around this clean little pussy, she felt her own power.

She sucked Jalisa's pussy until Jalisa kicked her away, panting and moaning, her labia engorged, her inner thighs slick with juice.

They turned, both at once, to check the oven clock.

"Shit," Jalisa said, sliding off the countertop, nearly falling to the floor because, clearly, Odessa had left her weak with orgasm. "I gotta get ready. I'm running so late."

That's when Odessa really started to sweat. The idea of being late didn't sit well with her. "I need to go, too. I've got a meeting."

Jalisa had already fled to the bedroom. Odessa made no further attempt at conversation. She slipped from her ex's condo and punched the elevator call button four thousand times.

The receptionist interrupted her reverie by saying, "I'll show you into the meeting room now."

When they arrived, the room was empty.

The receptionist had already walked halfway back to the waiting area when Odessa said, "Oh, sorry—hi? There's nobody here. I'm supposed to be meeting the Senior Accounts Manager. I don't have a name on file."

Turning, the receptionist tilted her head. "I meant to tell you Jalisa's running late."

Odessa's stomach dropped. "Jalisa?"

The receptionist nodded before walking away.

When Odessa dropped into one of the white leather meeting room chairs, she felt as though she were floating. Did Jalisa realize they'd be meeting this morning? Or were they both unaware they'd be seeing each other, professionally?

Odessa cupped her hand over her mouth and smelled her breath.

Smelled like pussy.

She sat a little taller and waited for Jalisa to arrive.

Secret Mercy

It happens when we fear there's nothing special about us: we allow our secrets to make us special. With our secrets, we set ourselves apart from the crowd. And when the secrets we're hiding are known by all, or when we realize our misdeeds are so commonplace that our secrets aren't even all that remarkable, we set out to create new secrets. They make us feel important, unique. And the more insidious our secrets, the more distinctive we feel.

At nineteen, Mercedes thought she was the only woman of her kind, unparalleled in the civilized world, leading a life of opulent vulgarity. By twenty-three, she'd realized she wasn't the only girl in the world to sleep with a married man. Nor, even, was she the only sweet young thing to take up with a man in his fifties.

It happened all the time.

She saw these couples on the street: the girl in the summer dress clinging to the silver fox in Dockers shorts, forgiving him the hideous socks-and-sandals combination.

"But I was in love with Simon," she repeated to herself, like a mantra meditation. "That girl with the French manicure and the blue shimmer eye shadow is only after the old guy's money, and he can only get it up for that tight piece of veal."

Cruel, to have these thoughts. Isn't it funny how something can be perfectly acceptable when *you* do it, but terribly atrocious when other people do?

Not that Mercedes thought all that much about Simon anymore.

On some unconfirmed date next spring or maybe summer, she'd be marrying Anwar: young, energetic and distinctly NOT already married to somebody else.

Simon could weave his own twisted way through life, because Mercy was taken.

Okay, so maybe Anwar wasn't always the generous, slow-going lover Simon had been, but he would learn. She'd have years to teach him, once they were married.

Years and years and years and years and years...

It wasn't only men who thought about sex every three seconds.

And, really, how could anybody survive the wait at the passport office without imagining a lover's hand squeezing her ass as he left a trail of kisses down her neck? Pioneering through the buttons of her blouse until his tongue was buried in her bra, searching for those straining buds...

"Mercedes," someone said, a pronounced baritone from long ago. "Mercy? I said your name three times. Where were you?"

Was it really him? Her heart leapt in her chest, and before she knew it her hand lay there trying to keep it in.

Act casual, stupid!

"Simon," she said, flustered and unable to disguise it. "I was just thinking about you..."

Wrong kind of casual, but Mercedes always was hopeless with deceit. Not because she couldn't deal out total bull. She could if the need arose. Mercedes simply preferred devastating honesty over a honey-glazed pack of lies.

Anyway, it was Simon's mouth she'd been imagining on a self-guided tour of her body.

His pink lips broke into a wide smile, reflecting her own, no doubt. He seemed flustered too, but did he ever look good! How many years since they'd...

"What are you doing here?" he asked.

Her insides were shivering like a naked Chihuahua, but rather than revealing her true colours, Mercedes slipped on her suit of sarcastic armour. "Well, I came in for pancakes, but then I realized this was a passport office, so I figure I'll get my passport renewed instead."

"Me too," he replied under strained laughter.

In the silence that followed, Mercedes weighed her options: go home unscathed to the man she was engaged to marry, or fuck her ex-lover's brains out in the bathroom of a passport office.

"They're calling your number, Mercy," Simon was saying.

"What? Oh. Right."

Her old nemesis, Doctor Disappointment, was back for a visit.

"Will you wait for me?" Simon asked.

Hey, after an extended holiday, it was her good friend Archduke Anticipation!

"You still married?" she asked.

"Yep," he replied, eyeing his toes.

"Remember how I said five years ago that I was done waiting for you?" Mercy taunted, though her tone didn't betray that she was teasing. She softened a little to say, "We'll see."

Of course she waited for him.

It was Simon, sexy Simon, four-time winner of the love-making World Cup.

Of course she waited.

"Gosh, I'm nervous," he admitted, joining her in the sterile government hallway.

"Gosh? You're such a five-year-old, Simon." She liked saying his name. "I'm getting married, you know."

He stared at the blank wall behind her head. Either he was off in space or he didn't hear her or he was so hurt he couldn't speak.

"I know," he finally replied.

Removing his glasses, he rubbed his eyes. Maybe he was crying. But who was he to be so wounded? He's the one who broke her heart, after all. No way would she feel sorry for him now. No way. Too late.

"Can we speak in private?" he asked.

Mercedes tried to suppress her excitement at the thought of being alone with Simon one more time. "Where?"

Like a lab rat, he looked in every direction for a way out of this government maze. Flustered again, he started walking—storming, more like—down the hallway and up a staircase.

Mercedes followed along, holding her skirts as she took the stairs by twos. Had she ever seen Simon so distressed? His energy was spinning, and she'd been sucked into it like some kind of lust tornado.

Energy conservation. No lights illuminated the next floor. It must have fallen into disuse, so Simon burst through the doorway, peeking into every room he passed. He must have found one that pleased him, because he went in. Manoeuvring his way around piles of chairs and disused office furniture, he made his way to the window overlooking Northern Willowdale.

"I don't want you to be offended," he said—an ominous beginning to any conversation.

Mercedes closed the office door. She climbed over a desk to get to him, wanting to throw her legs around his waist, but settling on standing at his knees as he sat on the cooling vent.

"Offended by what?" she asked.

"*What would I give to have you back in my life?*" he replied. "That's the question I've been asking myself since we broke up."

"Why would I be offended by that?"

He shook his head. "I'm desperately miserable without you, Mercy. Since you've been gone, I've realized your true worth. I've realized what a fool I was to let you slip away, and I've been trying to work up the courage to make you an offer."

Her heart quivered. "What kind of offer?"

Turning dramatically toward the window, he told her, "I can't bring myself to say it. You're going to hate me."

"Why? What's the offer?"

He turned to face her, but without looking her in the eye. "I had to ask myself this question: if your value translated into an actual dollar amount, what would that amount be? And I decided..." He fished his writing pad and pen from the front pocket of his shirt, then scrawled a figure.

Mercedes peeked over his arm to get a glimpse.

"That's it?" she shrieked. "That's all I'm worth to you? Less than a house? Or a car? Or a really good TV, even?"

Simon's cheeks turned deep pink as he explained, "No, no, no. This is what I'd be willing to pay you per..."

"Per...?"

"Per." He raised his eyebrows. Both of them. "*Per.*"

Holy crap, he wanted to pay her for sex.

And why would she be offended by an offer like that? He thought she was such an incredible fuck he'd be willing to give her cold, hard cash in exchange for something she'd already done a thousand times when they were together.

"Per what?" she pried, wanting him to say the word.

"Oh, I knew this was stupid," Simon said, shaking his head. "You're engaged and I'm on track to ruin it for you. Forget I said anything at all."

Mercedes grabbed hold of his wrist as he folded up his notepad. "Are you telling me you'd be willing to pay me *that much money* just to fuck your brains out once in a while?"

"I wouldn't have put it so crassly, but... well... I'd want it to be an ongoing thing. God, I hate myself for asking this of you. I just miss you, Mercy. I miss you so much."

"And you're not expecting me to leave Anwar for you," Mercedes confirmed, revelling in the wickedness of a new secret. "You just want me to screw you on the side?"

Simon looked so pathetic when he said, "How could I ask for anything more? I wouldn't leave my wife for you. Why should I expect you to leave your fiancé for me?"

The joke was on Simon. Mercedes would have fucked him for free. But, hey, if he wanted to throw his filthy money at her, so much the better. Today on Jerry Springer: *I'm a dirty whore and my fiancé doesn't have a clue!*

This was bad beyond bad. Big, bad Mercedes...

Running two bold hands up Simon's firm thighs, she whispered, "We've already wasted so many years..."

Mercedes never imagined she'd taste the sweet cherry aroma of Simon's mouth ever again. She'd forgotten the power of his tongue, how it snuck between her lips silent as a lamb, and in two shakes it was roaring like a lion.

She fought back, rough and tough against that hot body, running ecstatic hands down his back, squeezing those disappearing traces of love handles.

"Not a day goes by," she told him, "that I don't think about sucking your big, beautiful cock."

Simon stood, turning toward the door.

Mercedes clung tight to him. "Where are you going?"

"My butt's cold from sitting on the air conditioner," he replied, leaning instead against a solid oak desk.

With a smirk, Mercedes stood on her toes to kiss him. His erection throbbing against her abdomen. Oh, the sweet memories of that grateful cock!

Mercedes tore into Simon's shorts, sliding to her knees on the rough carpet. Her dress kissed the floor like a Christmas tree skirt while she dug out Simon's hard cock, letting its pink tip gloss her lips with precum.

That taste was like nothing else in the world, took her back years.

God, she'd missed Simon. You never get over your first love.

"Could you lick it like you used to?" Simon begged.

Mercedes knew just what he meant. Tracing circles around his cockhead with the tip of her tongue, she fondled his balls with one hand, flicking the seam of that soft and sensitive flesh with her thumb.

Simon's flesh leapt as he grasped the desk behind him. "Mercy, you're incredible!"

"You get what you pay for," she purred, meeting his gaze as she licked his cock like peppermint stick.

The lust in his eyes told her just how incredible she looked, tongue extended to meet his sweet rod. She licked. He shuddered.

"What now, Simon?"

Usually, he would have demurred and not answered at all. As a paying customer, he knew what he wanted.

"Suck it, Mercy. Take my cock in your mouth and suck it."

The string of naughty words made her pussy throb. She wrapped her hands around Simon's tight ass cheeks and ran circles around his incredible edible cock with her now-professional tongue.

What bad behaviour for a girl engaged to somebody else!

The very naughtiness of the situation made her tingle as Simon spoke words she'd never heard from the shy creature:

"Mercy, I want to fuck your throat."

That's one thing he'd never done when they were together, for fear of hurting her. But he was ready for it now, apparently. Mercedes could only respond with an eager growl, considering his dick was filling her mouth. Christ, he could fuck the hell out of her throat. He could make her sputter and gag, and she'd leave this room a happy hooker.

Slowly, Simon ran his cock against the silky walls of her mouth.

He took her head in his hands, sliding deeper inside.

Mercy relaxed to allow him entry. She squeezed his ass, sensing every gentle thrust of his hips as he plunged his beautiful body into her throat. God, was he big! How could she handle this wonderful assault, this dive into her oral depths?

As he ventured to thrust more forcefully, gripping her scalp in his powerful palms, it felt even better, more intense, more depraved. She was completely submissive, controlled by his whims.

Mercedes knew he was about to come when he started repeating her name endlessly: "Mercy, Mercy, Mercy."

With every utterance, Simon rammed her throat.

She gripped his fuzzy balls because she knew what that man liked.

Crying her name, tossing his head back, he came in her throat.

She took the opportunity to suckle his shrinking cock until his erection dwindled down to nothing.

Simon was still petting her hair when she let his penis fall from her lips.

God, was she wet.

"I trust my work was satisfactory," she said, teasing him.

"Highly," Simon replied, pulling up his shorts to find his wallet.

After brushing the carpet indentations from her knees, Mercedes stood before him, holding out her palm like Judy Jetson while Simon counted big bills. Was it possible this financial transaction was even more exhilarating than the throat-fucking?

Christ, it wasn't often she saw the value of her sexual self in cold, hard cash.

Tucking the bills into her bra, she leapt over the solid oak desk, making her escape. Simon was calling her name, but she couldn't turn to look at him.

She couldn't stay to chat because of the hot tears streaming down her cheeks.

Most upsetting of all was the fact that she knew she'd do it again.

She'd do it again and again and again and again.

After all, she needed a new secret. And this was a good one.

Capture the Bride

1

THE GIRLS ALL CHEERED when Sandra raised another glass. "To Tessa!"

"To Tessa!"

"To me!" Tessa clinked every champagne flute at the table, then gulped down her drink.

Bubbles rose in Tessa's throat and tickled her belly while Jillian grabbed her arm. "I can't believe you're getting married! It's so exciting!"

When Jillian started tearing up, Piri rolled her eyes. "Not this again. Enough with the waterworks, Jill. It's Tessa who should be crying."

The table fell silent. Most of the girls set down their glasses. Sandra cleared her throat and Jillian let go of Tessa's arm.

Sure Piri wasn't Sean's biggest fan, but why cause trouble now? This was supposed to be a bachelorette party! It was supposed to be fun!

"Hey," Sandra said, in a cheery tone that sounded kind of fake. "I almost forgot: I brought a little present for the bride-to-be."

Sandra pulled a plastic tiara out of her bag and set it on Tessa's head.

"Don't mess up her hair!" Fina cried.

"Right," Sandra shot back. "From this day forward, only Sean is allowed to mess up Tessa's hair."

There were lots of ooohs and kissy noises around the bar table. Truth be told, Tessa found the attention embarrassing. She'd much rather fade into the background.

God, she was nervous about the wedding. Having to stand up in front of all those people and say her vows? Hopefully all eyes would be on Sean. He'd sure look suave in his suit. Sean always looked suave. He was so attractive he turned Tessa's mind to mush. She couldn't think straight when he was around.

As the girls taunted Tessa, making suggestive remarks about her wedding night, the DJ kicked it into high gear, turning the lounge into a dance party.

Piri was the first to get up.

"Where are you going?" Sandra asked.

Pointing across the room, Piri said, "I've got my eyes on that prize over there."

Jillian looked to a dark-haired girl in a sequined dress. "Piri! This isn't a lesbian club."

Piri raised an eyebrow and said, "Every club is a lesbian club if you hit on the right girl."

Everyone watched as butch Piri strutted her big black boots across the lounge. Tessa felt like she was watching a train wreck in slow motion, until the girl in the sequined dress nodded slyly and handed her drink off to a friend.

"Holy crap," Sandra said. "I can't believe that worked."

"I'm gonna give it a shot," Fina said, rising from the table. "Piri makes it look easy."

"You're into girls now?" Tessa asked.

Hiking her tight skirt up her slim thighs, Fina said, "No, I want to see how many guys I can attract."

"Sounds like fun," Jillian said, hopping down from her bar stool. "Wait for me!"

"Best of luck," Sandra shouted, waving goodbye to the girls like they'd never see each other again.

Tessa sighed. "And then there were two."

Sandra tilted her head and smiled in a way that seemed to say, "What's eating you, kid?"

"I need to tell you something." Tessa looked over her shoulder to make sure Piri wasn't around to hear. "Alec came to see me a couple days ago."

"Say *what*?" Sandra hit Tessa's shoulder so hard it hurt. "And you're just telling me now?"

"I'm sorry," Tessa said, rubbing the spot where she'd been struck. "It didn't seem like a big deal at the time."

"Your ex-boyfriend comes to see you the week before your wedding and you think that's no big deal?"

"Keep your voice down. I don't want the others to know."

"Why not?" Suddenly, Sandra's eyes widened and she covered her mouth with both hands. "Don't tell me you hooked up!"

"No, Sandra!" This time it was Tessa doing the smacking. "I would never do a thing like that. Sean would kill me, for starters."

Sandra flinched.

"Not for real, obviously. He'd just be really mad. You know what he's like. I'm his girl."

"Right. Sure." Glancing toward the dance floor, Sandra said, "But it's not like you're married yet. If you wanted to give it one last go with Alec... or anyone..."

Tessa was really surprised to hear Sandra say a thing like that. "I'm engaged. I can't just sleep with random guys."

"No, not random guys. But Alec..."

"I'm engaged to *Sean*. I'm about to marry *Sean*. I'm not going to sleep with my ex-boyfriend days before my wedding. What are you thinking?"

"I'm thinking..." Sandra looked around too. "Tess, I never told you this, but I slept with another guy before I married Dante."

"More than one, I thought."

"No, no, I mean..." She looked a little shifty, but then took in a deep breath and gained an air of inflated pride. "My hometown boyfriend. My high school boyfriend. We invited him to the wedding."

Tessa felt like she'd been hit with a frying pan. "And you had sex with him?"

Sticking out her chest, Sandra said, "The night before the wedding."

"Jesus Christ! I'd expect something like that from Piri, but not from you. You're a pillar of morality, Sandra. I've always looked up to you for that."

"Right. And I wasn't married yet, so it's not a big deal. We got all those what-ifs out of our systems and I knew Dante was the man for me."

"So the sex wasn't great?" Tessa asked, scrunching up her nose.

Sandra grabbed her champagne flute and laughed. "The sex was amazing, but that's beside the point."

"If you say so." Tessa took another swig of champagne, and found she felt less judgemental with more alcohol in her system.

They turned to the dance floor and watched Jillian and Fina attracting men while Piri gripped that gorgeous girl's butt.

"I don't know what they see in her," Tessa said. Piri was one of her oldest friends, but they didn't have much in common. Still, it was just nice to keep in touch with someone who'd been in her life since before her parents died. She tended to tell Sandra more because Sandra listened and didn't judge, but Piri definitely knew her better than anyone.

That's why it bugged Tessa that Piri hated her fiancé.

"Sandra," she said without peeling her gaze from the dance floor. "You think Sean's a good guy, right?"

When Sandra didn't answer, Tessa convinced herself her friend simply hadn't heard the question. The music was getting really loud. That was a reasonable explanation.

2

"**H**ey!" Sandra cried, tapping Tessa on the shoulder. "You never told me why Alec came to see you."

"Shhh!"

Was Tessa seeing things, or had Piri turned when Sandra said that?

Tessa slid down from her bar stool and grabbed her purse off the table. "Come with me."

"Come where?" Sandra asked, grabbing her bag too.

"Somewhere quiet."

There was nowhere quiet, except the alcove in the hallway by the entrance. By the time they got there, Sandra was shivering from the draft. "What's got into you?"

"He begged me not to marry Sean."

"Who did?"

"Alec! Who did you ask about? Alec came to my office and said he needed to talk to me and, wouldn't you know, he told me I'd be an idiot to marry a man like Sean!"

Sandra finally looked as surprised as Tessa was hoping she would. "He called you an idiot? That doesn't sound like Alec."

"Well, those weren't his exact words," Tessa admitted. "I'm paraphrasing."

"I see."

"But he told me he'd found out all these terrible things about my fiancé!"

"What kind of terrible things?"

"I don't know. He didn't explain. He just said that if I didn't break it off he'd be forced to take drastic measures."

Pressing a hand to her chest, Sandra said, "You think he'll burst into the church when the minister asks if anyone knows a reason why this couple shouldn't wed?"

"I don't know," Tessa said. "Alec was always so shy. That's one of the reasons things fell apart between us. I wanted a guy who could take control, and Alec never could."

Sandra rubbed her arm sympathetically. "You really think he'd stand up in front of all those people and say... say what?"

Tessa shook her head. "I wish I knew. What dirt could he possibly have on Sean?"

Sandra didn't answer that question. She did shiver, though, obviously feeling the draft more profoundly with that thin frame.

"Go back inside," Tessa said.

"No, no. I'm fine."

"You're freezing! Go back in."

Sandra gave her a grateful smile, then asked, "Where are you headed?"

"I just need some air. I'll be back in a minute."

"Don't go far," Sandra said. "Stay where the bouncer can see you."

Tessa laughed. "I'm a big girl. I can take care of myself."

She gave Sandra a hug and felt the cold on her skin, then pushed her inside to warm up. After that, she walked into a crowd of people mostly younger than herself, though not by much. They were all waiting patiently to get into the club.

The air outside felt warmer than where she'd been standing with Sandra. The night felt not only hot, but wet. The city insisted on leaving a greasy film on her skin. Maybe it was the building itself. Maybe she was standing too close to lights or vents or something.

Sandra had warned her to stay where the bouncer could see her, but the sidewalk was crowded with young people eager to party. She wished she'd brought a pashmina to cover her naked shoulders. And another to cover her exposed thighs! She didn't usually wear heels, but her legs felt extra long tonight, and she wondered if she wasn't giving the wrong impression in this sleeveless mini-dress. She was about to get married, after all.

Two more sleeps and she'd be someone's wife. Hard to believe.

Taking off her tiara, she walked past a crowd of rowdy boys, ignoring their come-ons. Didn't they know she was engaged? Look! A ring! How dare they make such lewd suggestions?

Even once she'd gone past them, she could still feel their eyes on her flesh. They made her feel slimy and cheap. It was a horrid sensation, and she shivered just thinking about all the tawdry things they would do to her if they got her alone.

She walked a little faster, wishing she had Sean by her side. He was such an imposing presence. No man would dare to hit on her with him around.

When she turned to make sure those dirty boys had cleared off, she crashed into a stranger on the sidewalk.

Feeling terribly embarrassed, she said, "Oh goodness, I'm sorry."

"Had a little too much to drink, eh?"

She felt flustered and hot as she gazed up at the very tall man. He had a preppy look about him, with that plastic hair and polo shirt. Something in his eyes made her wary, and she wondered if maybe she'd drunk a little too much champagne.

Backing away, she said, "I'm fine. It was just... these boys, I wanted to make sure they..."

"You shouldn't be out here alone."

God, those eyes. They were maniacal, those eyes.

"I'm not alone," Tessa said. "My friends are in the club."

But the club was nearly a block away. Why had she walked so far? Why had she gotten out of the bouncer's sight-lines?

"Why don't I drive you home?" the guy asked, grabbing her wrist. "Come on. My car's right over here."

"No," she said, panicking so hard her legs wouldn't follow her brain's instructions to run, run far away! "No, I'm fine. My friends will wonder where I am."

"Don't want you drinking and driving."

"I'm not drinking and driving. Let me go!"

He wouldn't release her wrist, and she thought about kicking him in the shin, but if she raised one foot off the ground, would the other support her?

"I don't want a ride." She whimpered when she meant to shout. Her body wouldn't listen.

Just as the preppy guy pushed her against the car, another man came racing up to them.

What fresh hell is this?

3

But it wasn't hell at all. It was an angel come to save her by saying, "Hey! Get your hands off my fiancé!"

That's all it took for the preppy guy to release his hold. Just some other guy on the street.

"Are you okay, Tessa?" her saviour asked.

"No, I'm not okay. This guy was trying to get me in his car."

"Honest misunderstanding," the preppy guy said, putting his hands in the air as he walked to the driver's side.

He took off with his tail between his legs, leaving Tessa to throw her arms around her angel's shoulders. She was shaking when she said, "Alec, thank goodness for you! I was so scared. He wouldn't let go."

When her ex-boyfriend held her tight, she melted against him. She'd forgotten, until the other day, how wonderful it felt to be around the man. They had a special energy between them, something she'd never felt with anyone else.

She forced herself to pull back and ask, "What are you doing here?"

"You told me the other day."

Now she was really confused. "Told you what?"

"Where you were having your bachelorette party."

She laughed, still feeling high after being saved from heaven knows what fate. "It wasn't an invitation, Alec."

"I know." He set a gentle hand on her bare shoulder and led her back up the street. "But I need to talk to you."

She groaned without really meaning to. "We already discussed this, Alec. I'm marrying Sean and that's final."

"Final?"

"Final."

He shrugged. "Okay. That's all I needed to hear."

She lost a bit of respect for him every time he gave up so easily, but it still moved her that he cared. "Thanks for being concerned. It's good to know I've got someone in my court."

He nodded casually and looked around. "Say, I've got a little wedding present for you in my car, but I had to park around the corner."

She was about to tell him to send it to her new address, but what would Sean say? A gift from an old boyfriend would set him off for sure. Sean would ask if they'd seen each other recently, and she'd either have to lie or face his sullen jealousy.

"Okay," she told Alec. "That's sweet of you. Thanks."

He led her up the block, just past the club entrance, and then around the corner. When they got to his car—a sharp new sedan, much more sophisticated than the old clunker he drove when they were together—he opened the back door and pulled out a black fabric bag. Looked like the sort of thing you'd carry a nice pair of shoes around in.

"What's this?" she asked.

He reached inside and pulled out her present, then slung the bag over his shoulder.

She laughed. "You've got to be kidding me. What's this, a gag gift?"

"Not a gag," he said, gazing down at the length of rope.

He still had a smile on his face when he turned her around and pushed her against the car. She laughed, but asked, "What's this all about?"

"Sorry to take such drastic measures." Yanking both hands behind her back, he looped the black satin rope around her wrists. "You've left me very little choice, Tessa. You wouldn't listen to reason."

Was he serious?

He pulled the rope tighter and knotted it, pinching her skin. Up until that moment, she could take this as a joke. But as she listened to her ex's heavy breathing and felt the intensity of his restraints, she had to believe this was for real.

"Alec," she said. "What is wrong with you? Untie me now! Let me go!"

"Shh-shh-shh! Keep your voice down."

"Keep my voice down? You're tying me up and telling me to keep my voice down?"

"Trust me. This is a last resort—and I'll stop at nothing to protect you."

"Protect me?" she cried. "I need to be protected *from* you!"

She looked around, wondering why nobody had come to her rescue, but this little side street was totally void of pedestrians. All the shops were dark, and most of them boarded up. Jeeze, this wasn't a very nice neighbourhood, was it?

Trying to keep it together, she said, "Alec, if you don't untie my right now I'll scream bloody murder."

"I thought you might say that." He shoved the black bag over her head and then folded her body down, pushing her into the back seat of his car. "Sorry about all this. I really am."

"Alec!" she cried as the panic of darkness set in. "Alec, I don't understand. Why are you doing this to me?"

He slammed the car door, whacking the bottoms of her shoes. She kicked off her heels, then went at the door with the pads of her feet. A lot of good that would do. She kicked the seat in front of her instead. Her toes landed against the upholstery, but at least that didn't hurt.

Anyway, this had to be some kind of joke. Not a very funny one, but a joke nonetheless.

Maybe Sandra had put him up to this. Or Piri. She had a sick sense of humour at times.

When Alec got into the driver's side, he said, "Comfy?"

"Comfy? Are you kidding me? What is wrong with you? Tell me the truth: was this Piri's idea?"

"All mine," he said as he started up the engine. "I'm sorry to have to do it, but desperate times call for desperate measures."

"What's that supposed to mean?"

As he pulled out onto the road, he said, "I can't let you marry that man."

"It's not your decision, Alec!"

"Well... I disagree."

Tessa couldn't get over how reasoned he was with all this. He had an answer for everything.

So she asked him, "Why did you tie me up?"

"Because I can't let you go to your wedding."

"It's *my* wedding. I kind of have to be there."

"I can't let you do that, Tessa."

"You can't just abduct me."

He sped through the downtown streets at a time when only taxis and maniacs were on the road. With an ominous laugh, he said, "Oh, Tessa. Sweet, kind, darling Tessa. I'm afraid I already have..."

4

All the kicking and screaming in the car must have tired Tessa out, because she had no memory of Alec's vehicle coming to a stop. When she woke up the next morning, she didn't know where she was or how she'd gotten there.

At least he'd taken the bag off her head. It would have been nice if he'd untied her, but no such luck. When she shifted on the bed, she realized her ankles were bound with the same silky black rope as her wrists.

How had she managed to sleep with both hands behind her back? She must have drunk considerably more champagne than she'd thought.

That, or he'd drugged her.

No. No, Alec would never do a thing like that.

Then again, she'd have sworn he would never do a thing like this either: abduct her off the street, bring her to this dank motel room—she could only assume it was a motel room. She knew for sure it was dank.

When she thought about being shoved into the back seat of his car, she didn't remember being particularly frightened. It was more like an adventure. This was Alec! He wouldn't hurt a fly. If he insisted on tying her up and kidnapping her, he must have a good reason for it.

But what if that wasn't the case?

Maybe Alec had changed in the time they'd been apart. Maybe their breakup had turned him into a monster. Maybe his love for her had festered, and her impending nuptials had triggered something horrendous in his psyche. Isn't that what they talked about on *Criminal Minds*? A trigger: an event that catapults a normal person into doing something horrible? Maybe that's what happened to Alec.

Maybe he was capable of horrible things. Maybe she should have fought back when he shoved her against the car. When he tied her up. When he abducted her...

A strange feeling took over, like she had a giant ice cube in her chest and it was melting slowly... slowly. She felt each drip like an autumn chill in her belly.

That's when she realized this wasn't all fun and games. They weren't playing a round of Capture the Bride.

This was for real.

The door opened and Tessa struggled to arch up from the bed. Her head felt like a bowling ball, too heavy to lift. The only sound in her ears was her heartbeat, and it roared like thunder. She couldn't even hear Alec's footfalls as he approached the bed.

How did she know it was Alec? Oh, she knew. They'd been together long enough that she still remembered the refined musk of his skin. That scent filled the air, cutting through the dank odour of the motel room and, she now realized, the smell of sweat and alcohol that had become her own perfume.

"Good morning, Sunshine."

Tessa steeled at the sound of his voice. It was like a drizzle of hot caramel on her cool apple skin. Part of her wanted to wade into it like a sun-kissed pool, but she forced herself to resist.

"You were out like a light," he said. "Sleep well?"

"Did you drug me?" she asked.

He chuckled heartily, then told her, "I didn't have to drug you. But I would have, if it came to that. Anything to keep you from marrying a monster."

She kicked her feet, forgetting they were restrained, causing herself to flop hopelessly on the bed. "I hate you for doing this. I hate for bringing me here!"

Once she'd screamed at him, she regretted it in the extreme. Her throat went raw. That's all it took: a few I hate yous and a scream, and her throat felt sliced and dry.

"I need water," she told him, croaking out the words. "Give me water."

He came closer, right next to the bed, and finally she could see his face: slightly scruffy, bright blue eyes, dark gleaming hair. She'd always been a fan of that cleft chin, and there was something about his nose that made her suddenly love noses. Who ever heard of an attractive nose? But Alec had one, from any angle.

When he reached for her, she went to smack him before remembering her wrists were bound behind her. "What are you doing? Don't touch me!"

Her screams came out alluringly husky.

"Spare me the conniption," he said. "I'm taking you to the bathroom. I assume you have to pee."

"No," she shot back, but he was right, of course. Now that she thought about it, she needed desperately to go. So she said, "Fine. For you."

He laughed as he turned her on the bed. "You're going to pee just for me?"

She didn't answer. She just let him take her weight, pressing her face against his chest as her feet met the floor. He led the way, somewhat carrying her while she hopped toward the bathroom—which took dank to new heights.

"You have to take my panties down," she whispered to him.

This was far too intimate, even for people who'd been close in bygone days.

While she stood in the turquoise tiled room, he hiked up her clingy club dress and then peeled down her skimpy thong.

"Take it off," she said. "All the way off. I don't want to wear it anymore."

Alec got down on the floor and slowly brought the thong down her thighs, then past her knees. It stuck at her ankles, where the ropes bound her tight. He didn't seem to notice that he couldn't complete his task. Not now that he'd come face to face with the place he'd known so well, once upon a time.

She'd gone all out for the wedding night, waxed to the nines for her groom. Sean preferred her to be hairless, or at least to keep it minimal. In fact, any time she let it grow out too much he teased her relentlessly, called her Woolly Mammoth. That was his sense of humour. Not one she particularly shared, but man and wife didn't need to agree about everything. If they did, no one would ever get married.

"Take it off," she told Alec, hoping he'd trust her enough to unravel those ropes around her ankles.

When he gazed up at her, the smirk on his face made her simultaneously weak-kneed and pissed off. She couldn't decide if his expression was smarmy or sincere when he asked, "Are you sure about this?"

"Take it off," she said.

And that's precisely what he did: wrapped his hands around one side of her thong and pulled until it snapped. The force knocked her back, and she landed with her butt on the toilet seat. On impulse, she started to pee. She couldn't help herself. It was a reflex, and one that embarrassed her tremendously.

She tried to stop, but there was no use. Her body took the reins and she peed while Alec tore apart the other side of her thong. Once he'd completed that task, he rose to his feet and watched her go.

"Remember the first time you peed in front of me?" he asked. "We were at your place, mid-conversation. You'd made me dinner that night and we were watching TV. You got up from the couch, went to the bathroom, and you didn't close the door once you were in there. Pushed down your jeans, pulled down your panties, and you were off to the races."

The memory struck her hard in the heart. "I didn't realize what I was doing," she said. "It was like you weren't there. But you were. Like you were just another part of me. It's hard to explain."

"But easy to understand," he assured her. "Because I felt the same way about you. Still do."

Her heart fluttered before she could catch the sensation and tamp it down. "You can't tell me things like that, Alec. I'm about to get married."

His expression hardened. "Not if I can help it."

5

Any long-held love she'd kept in her heart hardened when she remembered what he'd stolen her away from. "This isn't funny, Alec. You need to let me go. My friends probably called the cops when I didn't come back to the club last night. Did you think of that?"

"Yup."

"You thought of everything, huh?"

"Yup."

She reached for the toilet paper before remembering her hands were tied behind her back. Great! Now how was she supposed to manage? Especially when Alec spun on his heels and left her alone in the bathroom.

As much as she didn't want to be with him, she didn't want to be alone either. "Alec? Where are you going? You can't just leave me here!"

He returned with her phone and showed her the screen: Sandra's texts from the night before, asking where she'd gone off to—and her reply that she'd gone home early to think about things.

"What things?" Sandra had texted.

"Wedding things," Tessa had apparently texted back. "TTYL."

Tessa looked up at Alec. That was definitely a smarmy look on his face. Or a concerned one. She couldn't decide. "You sent that?"

He nodded.

"You texted my friend?"

"I always liked Sandra," Alec said. "She has a good head on her shoulders."

Tessa almost spilled the beans, like she would have in the good old days. She almost said, "You won't believe what Sandra told me! The night before her wedding, she slept with her old boyfriend!"

In fact, she really wanted to tell him, now that the thought had sprung to mind. But that would show weakness on her part. It would show she still thought of him as the guy she could tell everything. Even hush-hush best friend gossip.

And he wasn't that guy anymore. Sean was.

Or... should be.

In truth, there was a lot she didn't tell Sean. He didn't seem to like any of her friends. Hated Piri. Hated all lesbians, in fact. Anyone gay. Anyone different. Hated poor people, thought they were lazy. Hated artists, same reason.

The list went on.

Tessa really wanted Sean to like Sandra, but he didn't. At first, she'd wondered if it was because of Sandra's skin colour, but she soon realized it wasn't just Black people he had it in for.

In a weird way, the fact that Sean hated everyone made Tessa feel special. Cherished. He must have seen something super-impressive in her. Sometimes she wondered what. She didn't feel super-impressive, or even slightly impressive. She'd always felt just a little bit fatter, a little less well-maintained, maybe a little uglier than all those other girls.

Once, long ago, she'd confided these thoughts to Alec. He'd told her, "Audrey Hepburn worried that she was ugly too."

That still made her smile.

"I have a special guest I'd like you to meet," Alec said from somewhere outside.

"Great! Perfect! Just what I need." When Alec entered the bathroom, Tessa looked up at him from her seat on the throne. "Should we all conference in here? Bring your friends. It'll be a party."

"Oh," he said, glancing at the toilet paper roll. "I guess you can't..."

"No, I can't."

"Would you like me to...?"

"No!" she shouted. "God, I need a drink of water."

"I'll get you some. But first..."

Sighing, Tessa parted her legs as much as she could, considering they were tied together at the ankles. "Fine, go ahead. It's nothing you haven't seen before."

"Or touched," he said. "Or licked or..."

"Okay! Enough." She glanced up at him as he reached for the toilet paper, pulling ample wads off the roll. The scent of his skin was all around her, making her senses spin like a top. "Enough."

All at once, she was back in time, spreading her legs while her boyfriend went down on her. She could still see Alec kneeling beside the bed while she perched on her elbows. She always did like watching him work.

Of course, at a certain point she would have to close her eyes. She had this strange unfounded fear that if she came with her eyes open, they'd explode. So, really, she had to close her eyes on multiple occasions, with Alec.

She almost never had to close them with Sean.

But they could work on that. Once they were married, the bedroom stuff would surely improve.

Tessa had to laugh at the sheer quantity of toilet paper Alec had unravelled from the roll. He used it like a puffball to pat her most intimate parts. She tried to ignore the light pressure he exerted, and the feathery touch of that soft paper against her satin skin.

"Good?" he asked.

It felt more than good, but no way she'd tell him that. She nodded, then asked, "Who's my special guest? Is it Piri? Did you set this up between you? She never liked Sean."

Lifting her off the throne, he said, "No, it's not Piri."

"Is it Sandra? Don't tell me it's Sandra."

"It isn't Sandra."

"Not Jillian..."

"It's no one you know," he said, pulling her clingy dress down to cover her butt.

When he didn't say anything more, she asked, "Well? Who is it?"

6

He helped her back into the motel room, and she looked around. She hadn't taken proper note of her surroundings when she'd been flat on her back, but now she gazed from the bare mattress to the 70s-era dresser to the curtains that looked like they'd been dug out of some old lady's trash bin. They blocked out not only the sunshine but also the window itself. How big was it? Could she fit through? Were there bars keeping her inside?

She should really be planning her escape. If Alec wouldn't release her, she'd have to set herself free. After all, she was getting married the following day.

There was a light fixture near the opposite end of the room—a bulb loosely concealed by some kind of dark wicker shade. Underneath was a small round table and two chairs sitting dangerously close to the door. Alec led her in that direction and sat her down in one of the chairs. It wasn't very comfortable, but it was better than standing.

"Can't you undo my wrists?" she asked. "I promise I won't escape."

He laughed in a way that was uncharacteristically smug, and said, "You don't have to promise me you won't escape. I'll make goddamn sure you don't."

There was the faintest sense of threat in those words. In fact, coming from anyone but Alec, the threat would have been major. Looming. Frightening as hell.

Years ago, she'd never have imagined she might one day need to overpower him. Looking at him now, in that fitted black long-sleeved T and those dark blue jeans, she knew she couldn't.

Why had she never noticed those muscles before? Did he not have them when they were dating? Or had she simply overlooked them because he was such a nice guy? Nice guys didn't need to use their muscles—certainly not with the women they loved.

"Lean forward," he said, and she did without question.

He untied her wrists and let her shake out her hands. "Ohhh that feels good!"

If she played her cards right, she'd be able to dart toward that door the second he seemed distracted.

"Thanks for trusting me," she said, batting her eyelashes, acting all compliant.

"Oh, I don't trust you, Tessa. I don't trust you in the least."

What came next was a frenzied blur. Before she knew what was happening, her forearms were tied to the armrests. How did he do that? She was secured once again, this time to the chair. What was he going to do next? Tie her ankles to the table legs?

"Alec," she said, feeling truly scandalized. "Why are you doing this to me? This isn't you. You were never the jealous type."

"Nothing to do with jealousy, Tessa."

"Well, what is it, then? And where's my water?"

"Our special guest is bringing the water," he said. "And once you've heard what she's got to say, you'll understand why I brought you here. Why I can't let you marry Sean."

There was a quiet knock at the door and Alec made his way over. All those security latches would surely trip up Tessa when she eventually made a run for it.

She could just see herself hopping along the highway, trying to hitchhike in club wear and no panties... with a motel chair strapped to her butt.

Once he'd dealt with the latches, Alec opened the door just a crack. Tessa watched the expression on his face for clues as to who this might be, but she couldn't read it well enough to know.

As he opened the door yet wider, he said, "Denise. Thank you for coming. I'd like you to meet my good friend, Tessa."

When the woman named Denise walked in, the first thing Tessa focused on was the three bottles of water she hugged to her chest. Not the sleek tan trousers or the cute ruby shoes or the neat knit sweater set. That came after.

But it wasn't until Tessa looked Denise in the face that she got a sinking feeling as to why this woman was here. Tessa had never seen anything like it, except on TV. Denise's skin was mottled with glossy, wax-like patches. One eye looked fearful but loving, and Tessa tried to concentrate on it to keep from staring at the empty space where her other eye should have been.

"Tessa," Alec said. "I'd like you to meet Denise—your fiancé's first wife."

7

"Sean told me about you," Tessa said, feeling conflicted about this woman's presence. "The way he talked, I thought you'd be more..."

She didn't know how to finish that sentence without sounding hopelessly insulting. Sean had always characterized his first wife as a gold-digging tramp who slept with every man under the sun. Tessa couldn't imagine many men wanting a woman with a face like that. She felt like a terrible person just thinking that thought, but most guys didn't go for horribly disfigured girls.

"I brought you some water," Denise said, placing the bottles on the table.

Alec closed the door and started in on those locks. "Thanks again for coming," he said.

"No thanks needed. I'd do anything to keep another woman from going through what I did."

Denise didn't seem shocked by Tessa's slatternly appearance, much less the fact that she was tied to a chair. She turned the lid on one of the bottles and Tessa heard the snap of the safety plastic. Otherwise she'd have wondered if this woman was about to drug her.

"Tilt your head back and open your mouth."

In any other context, that request would have sounded dirty, but Tessa was too desperate for hydration to think about things like that. She let the stranger pour cool water into her throat and swallowed it eagerly, gulp after gulp. Drips escaped the corners of her mouth and slid down her chin, soaking the front of her dress. She didn't care. She needed this.

Denise petted her hair gently, then slowly backed away. "Let me know when you want another sip."

"Okay."

"Should I leave you two alone?" Alec asked.

Denise took a seat in the second chair and said, "No, stay with us. It's nothing you haven't heard before."

"Are you two... dating?" Tessa asked. "Are you a couple?"

When Denise smiled, only half her mouth took part. The other half remained frozen, looking tight, like plastic wrap. "No," she said. "We met by chance. A happy accident. Alec has known my story for a long while, but when I told him the name..."

"I couldn't believe it," Alec jumped in. "I felt like I'd been punched in the gut."

Tessa looked from one to the other. "I have no idea what you're talking about."

"My ex-husband," Denise said. "The man you're about to marry. Who do you think did this to me?"

Denise touched her fingers to her face as she told Tessa how it happened. She'd been in the kitchen. "Once we were married, Sean told me my place was in the kitchen. The kitchen or the bedroom. That was it."

Tessa bit back, "Sean would never say a thing like that. Never."

Rather than arguing, Denise remained momentarily silent. Then she said, "I had a big pot of potatoes boiling away on the stove. Sean always loved his mashed potatoes."

That was true. Potatoes and gravy.

"Potatoes and gravy," Denise went on. "I'm cooking his dinner and the phone rings and I answer. It's a telemarketer. They always call at the worst possible moment."

Alec laughed. "That's true."

Denise obviously didn't hear him. She was focused on her story, like she was seeing it play out in front of her.

"Sean was standing in the doorway, watching me. We had this little galley kitchen and he liked to block me in like an animal in a cage. I say to this telemarketer that it's not convenient to talk. I'm too polite to tell anyone to shove off. I say goodbye and I hang up the phone, and suddenly Sean's right there in my face."

Tessa tried not to see it, but she couldn't look away. Denise had created a horror movie in her mind. It seemed so real.

"He's screaming at me, pulling my hair, asking *who was that on the phone? Your boyfriend?* I tell him it was just a telemarketer. He says he heard a man's voice. Am I fucking him? I ask: who, the telemarketer? He won't believe me. He's convinced, but I'm trying to calm him down because that's all I've done every second of every day since we got married. Just try to calm him down even though what he's saying is crazy."

Alec picked up a box of cheap motel tissues and brought them to the table. He didn't put his hand on Denise's shoulder, which is what Tessa would have done. He just put down the tissue box and walked back to the bed where he sat quietly, out of the way.

Denise let out a tiny sob, and then opened another bottle of water. Tessa stole a glance at her strange skin as she took a drink. Water spilled out the side of her mouth that didn't work properly, and she cleaned herself up with a tissue.

"I'm sorry," she said. "It never gets easier."

Tessa didn't know how to respond, so she didn't respond at all. She sat stiff as a board and tried not to breathe.

"He called me every name in the book," Denise said. "He had these ideas in his head, and how could I convince him? I couldn't. I was his woman, his property. He had to punish me. That's when he slammed my face into the potatoes, into the pot of boiling water."

"Oh my God," Tessa said, though she hadn't meant to speak.

"Lucky thing I turned my head just before my face hit the water. This side got the worst of it. If I hadn't turned I'd have lost both eyes. That's one thing I learned from all this: to be thankful for small mercies."

Tessa's stomach turned and turned, again and again, like a washing machine. It just wouldn't settle.

"Tell her what he told the police," Alec said.

Denise nodded, smiled somewhat. "When I was at the hospital, Sean told everyone I did it myself, I was crazy. I had third degree burns and he was telling them to release me. He was my husband. He would care for me at home."

Alec shook his head. "Good thing the hospital called the cops."

"I had this one nice nurse who held my hand, never let go, and I remember saying to her: I'd rather die than go back with that man. You either kill me or you find me a way out. And, small mercies, she knew what to do. But I was on the run for years. Make no mistake: death would have been the easy way out. This way? Nothing easy about it."

Tears pricked Tessa's eyes, but she blinked them back. Her stomach felt sour and so unsettled she worried she might vomit all over the industrial yellow carpet. It would blend right in.

She didn't want to seem insensitive, so she said, "I'm sorry about everything you went through, but there's no way we're talking about the same man. My Sean would never do those things—to you, to me, to anyone."

Alec stood abruptly from the bed. "Listen to what she's telling you, Tessa. Sean *did* do those things. And after Denise left him, he tracked her down. Everywhere she moved, he found her. He followed her."

"I came home to my new basement apartment and he'd scrawled *I'll kill you bitch* across the door. Try moving forward with your life when you spend every second looking over your shoulder."

Tessa got that same gut-punch sensation Alec had been talking about before. In the back of her mind, a voice was telling her to listen carefully, but she pushed it away and said, "I think we've got our wires crossed. There are plenty of Seans out there. Yours and mine are definitely not the same guy."

Denise rattled off every piece of personal information possible, all accurate, right down to the birth mark on his butt.

But the fact that this woman knew so much about her husband-to-be didn't scare Tessa—it only made her angry. "Look, I really am sorry someone hurt you but I don't know why you're dragging my fiancé into your mess. My Sean is a charming, handsome, romantic guy. He loves me and he wants to take care of me for the rest of my life. It sucks that your Sean was a piece of shit, but that doesn't mean mine is too."

Alec bolted across the room, forcing Tessa to look at him. "Don't you get it? Your Sean *is* her Sean. It's the same guy. What he did to her he *will* do to you, and I love you way too much to let that happen."

"What are you saying?" Tessa shot back. "If you can't have me no one can? Who's the abusive asshole now?"

Alec's jaw clenched. He marched toward the bed, then turned around to say, "Do I want you to be with me? Yes, of course I do. You're the only woman I've ever loved. I'll put that on the table right now."

"Don't marry Sean," Denise pleaded. Leaning forward, she petted Tessa's hand. "You know that feeling deep down in your gut? The one that's telling you there's something off about this guy? You need to listen to that feeling, Tessa. You need to listen now because, if you marry Sean, he *will* kill you."

8

Tessa fought them tooth and nail. She screamed and shouted, told them they were wrong, they didn't know Sean at all, he loved her and she loved him and Alec was just trying to steal her best chance at happiness. Denise and Alec took turns pouring water down her throat every time she got hoarse. The louder she grew, the quieter they became, like parents permitting their child a tantrum to tire herself out.

Denise had a quiet, calm answer for everything. Sean had bought Tessa expensive gifts? He'd bought Denise expensive gifts, too, when they were dating. After they were married he sold them out from under her to feed a poker habit that was apparently more important than their love.

Sean wrote Tessa poetry? Oh, so sweet. He'd done the same thing for Denise back in the day. The only poems he wrote her after they were married were death threats on doors. As for sweet nothings in her ear, those would turn into reminders like: "I own you, woman. My wife is my property. Ugly bitch. You're nothing without me."

Tessa kept insisting Sean would never say those things. He loved her. He would never raise a hand to her. Never.

But then why could she hear those words so clearly in her mind? Why did the voice she'd always found so alluring suddenly seem menacing in the extreme?

She couldn't imagine that the man she loved would turn into someone else after they married, but Denise kept insisting this was the case. It had happened before.

Denise sat on the bed next to Alec. "It makes you feel good at first."

Alec took her hand and squeezed. When Tessa saw his compassion for the woman, she allowed herself to mistake it for something more. A streak of jealousy coursed through her chest, like ice, but burning hot.

Still, when Alec didn't ask Denise what "makes you feel good at first," Tessa did.

Denise looked up, like she'd been lost in a dream—or maybe a nightmare. "His possessiveness," she said. "If he wants to own you, that means you're worth being owned. Makes you feel special."

The burning ice in Tessa's chest melted, because she knew just what Denise was talking about. When Sean held her close on the dance floor, she felt owned. And she loved it.

And when he threatened other men who dared to look at her, she felt like a princess. Finally, she'd found the one man who would stand up for her, fight for her.

But here was Denise saying that as soon as they got married, he wouldn't be fighting for her—he'd be fighting against her.

Tessa sat quietly with that thought while Denise rose from the bed. Heading to the door, she said, "I really hoped I could change your mind, but I can see I haven't made a dent." Tessa simply stared at the woman's shoes while she said, "Men like Sean... they don't stop at one."

When Tessa didn't respond, Denise got down on the ground and forced herself into Tessa's line of sight. She could hear the beauty in the woman's voice, but that face made her too sorrowful to speak.

She gazed into Denise's one remaining eye just as Denise said, "We won't let that man kill you."

The idea was so jarring Tessa lashed out. "Sean would never do that. He's a good person. He would never... never..."

Denise wouldn't listen to any excuses, which came as a relief because Tessa didn't feel like making them. Being tied to a chair was surprisingly exhausting. Or maybe it was the assault of information that rendered her so weary. Either way, she slumped in her seat while Denise left the room, each step pleading for Tessa to reconsider.

"I learned the hard way," Denise said as a parting shot. "You don't have to. You can make a different choice."

When she was gone, Alec gazed at Tessa like he was the school principal and she'd been up to no good. "Well?"

"Well what?" Tessa growled. "You bring in some crazy lady to say my fiancé's a maniac and you expect me to buy it? You think I'm that bad a judge of character?"

"Sean is an abuser. He manipulated you into thinking he's a good guy, but he's not. You heard Denise."

"Denise is a liar."

Alec groaned and pressed his palms against his eye sockets.

"I listened to your ridiculous accusations. Now let me loose! I'm getting married tomorrow." Tessa struggled against her bindings, feeling them loosen around her forearms. She slowed down, then, because she didn't want Alec seeing that she might be able to free herself.

"Tessa, listen to me: I can't let you marry this guy."

"Then you're just as bad as Denise says Sean is. No—you're worse! You kidnapped me!"

Her phone buzzed and they both looked toward the dresser, where it was sitting.

"Give me that!" she said.

He picked it up and looked at screen.

"Don't read my texts!" She squirmed in her seat. "Who is it? Sandra? My friends are looking for me, I bet. They're going to find me. They'll call the police. You won't get away with this, Alec!"

He shoved her phone in his back pocket, then said, "You haven't eaten anything today. I'll get us some food. Promise to stay put?"

Tessa wriggled her arms, feeling the slack in the rope and knowing it was loose enough that she could escape. Still, she said, "Where am I supposed to go? I'm tied to a chair, in case you've forgotten."

He gave her a dubious look before making his way to the door. "Okay. See you in a few, babe."

Babe. That's what he used to call her when they were a couple. He obviously hadn't meant to say it, but too late.

She was still his babe. After all this time.

9

When Alec left her alone, she sat very quietly to listen for his car.

He must have known she'd try to escape. Alec wasn't a stupid guy. If he left her alone, he must have expected her to wriggle out of her binds. They were so loose all she had to do was pull her arms out and, abracadabra, freedom!

Her hands felt weird, numb. She couldn't move her fingers properly. So instead of untying her ankles right away, she steadied herself against the walls and the furnishings while she hopped to the window. Finally, she would find out where he'd taken her.

But when she pulled open the curtains, she found the window boarded up from outside. That had to be why it was so quiet in here: whatever motel this was, it must have closed down. She tried to think of local motels that had gone out of business, but she really didn't keep track of those things.

Tessa tried again to untie her feet, but her hands were still numb. Hopefully she had a bit of time before Alec got back. The man had fine taste. When they were dating, he always treated her to nice meals. He'd have to drive a fair distance to find one around here—wherever "here" was.

She bounced to the door, flipped the deadbolt, took a deep breath, and opened it.

The hallway was black. Not the slightest sliver of illumination, except the light spilling out from her room. They must have cut power to this place when it closed down.

Wait. Her room had lights. How was that possible?

She turned and looked around. The lights were on. How had Alec managed that? He must have put a lot of thought and effort into this abduction.

Tessa started laughing when she realized how odd it was to admire her ex's kidnapping abilities.

Her laughter echoed through the darkened hallway, and the sound made her heart shudder. Then she realized the laughter continued without her. It wasn't an echo at all. Other voices joined in. Other voices, other rooms.

Other people?

Oh God, there were other people in the other rooms!

Tessa's heart raced and she slammed the door, securing every lock she could figure out.

Which was more imposing: the threat posed by Alec, or hysterical strangers in a darkened motel? By the way her heart pounded, she was leaning toward the latter.

This was unbelievable. Tomorrow was meant to be the happiest day of her life, and today she was trapped in a boarded-up motel room under threat of...

Threat of what?

Alec hadn't threatened her in any way. He just took her by force. Yes, that was bad. But he had a good reason for doing it—in his mind, at least. In his mind, he was saving her from a fate like Denise's.

Tessa leaned against the door for what felt like hours. Every time she blinked, she saw Denise's glossy skin and missing eye.

She heard the woman's warnings and fought them off in her mind.

Alec would never have done a thing like this if he hadn't been concerned for her safety and wellbeing. For her very life. He didn't want her dead any more than she wanted to die. That's why she unlocked the latches on the door, hopped back to the chair by the table and slid her arms back in the ropes, waiting for Alec's return.

"GREEK," HE SAID. "YOUR favourite."

She blushed, and not just because he'd remembered her favourite meal.

He set takeout containers on the table, then regarded her for a moment.

"What?" she asked.

"I'm just wondering if I can trust you not to run away."

If Alec untied her ropes, he'd feel how slack they'd gone. He'd realize she could have escaped when he was out, and that she'd chosen not to. And then he'd think all kinds of wrongheaded things. He'd think she wanted to be here with him instead of marrying Sean.

"The second you untie me, I'll beat you down, buddy. I'll break a chair over your back if I have to, and I know you won't fight back because you would never hit a woman. Not in a million years."

He didn't argue with her there. "Okay, then I'll feed you."

"Fine."

"There's a simple solution to all life's problems."

"Apparently."

He opened the takeout container to reveal her go-to meal: chicken souvlaki, mixed vegetables, rice, and... lemon potatoes.

She'd never been able to feel the colour drain out of her face before, but she certainly felt it as she stared down at those potatoes. Because they were more than just food. They were a cautionary tale painted in boiling water and galley kitchens.

Tessa closed her eyes, but that was even worse. She was right there, watching the man she was about to marry hover over this slight woman like a caged lion. The rage in his eyes scared her half to death, and when he reached for her hair she couldn't back away, couldn't move.

This time, it was Tessa's face that went into the pot. It was Tessa's skin that melted like candle wax. Tessa's eye that exploded from her head. Tessa screaming with a pain worse than anything she'd felt in her life.

"Shh! Shh! Shh! Tessa, what's wrong?"

When Alec wrapped his arms around her, she pulled out from the ropes and hugged him hard. Sobbing on his shoulder, she said, "I can't marry him, Alec. Why didn't I see it before?"

"It's okay, babe. I'm here."

"He'll kill me when I call off the wedding."

"I'm here, Tess."

"No, I mean it. That man will track me down. That's it. I'm dead."

"I'll protect you."

"You can't protect me forever," she said.

Alec pulled back just enough that she could look into his caring blue eyes. He said, "I can, Tessa. I *can* protect you. Forever."

She wasn't sure what came over her in that moment. Five minutes ago she'd been committed to marrying Sean. Now her pulse was racing for this man she used to know.

And he knew her. He knew her mind, her spirit... and her body.

Lifting her from the chair, he carried her to the bed and tossed her on top of the covers. She bounced as he reached for her ankles and untied the ropes. She still couldn't move her feet. Her arms and legs were dead weight.

If he wanted her, he'd have to take her.

10

"Don't," she said as he pulled off her dress. "I smell awful."

He jumped on top of her, fully clothed except for his shoes. "You smell amazing. Don't put yourself down."

"But it's true," she said, melting into the mattress as he moved his hands up the sides of her naked body. "I need a shower, Alec. Please let me shower?"

When he arched on top of her, she felt his hardness pressing down. Maybe she didn't need a shower after all. The swell of passion between her legs sure didn't care whether she was clean or dirty. In fact, the dirtier, the better.

But Alec hopped off the bed and said, "I'll let you shower on one condition: that I come with you."

"You'd *better* come with me."

His eyes bulged, and so did his bulge! She'd never seen his cock react so intently through his clothing. When they were together, she thought of him as the sweetest, kindest, most refined man on the planet.

In here, he was an animal growling for the pleasures of the flesh.

"My body feels so weak," she said. "Being tied up took so much out of me."

He tore off his top and said, "My body will have to be strong enough for the both of us."

Was Tessa imagining things, or had Alec gotten considerably more muscular since they were a couple? His abs rippled impressively as he unbuckled his belt, and again as he threw down his pants. Sean's hot body paled in comparison to Alec's strong thighs and impressive erection.

Just looking at his dick sent a streak of passion through her core. She pulsed between the legs, in time with the obvious throbbing of his cock.

When he swept in to lift her, she said, "Wait."

"I can't wait."

"No, Alec, this isn't right. I'm still engaged to Sean. I can't sleep with you."

"Even if you want to?"

Was it really that obvious? Her legs were slightly parted, after all. Could Alec see the wetness glistening all down her thighs? Her pussy wasn't shy about showing off its arousal. And her nipples couldn't possibly peak any harder. They were so tight they hurt.

"We can't do this," she told him as he rounded the bed, standing at the base with his hands on his hips. "Until I call off the wedding, I can't."

"You've called it off in your heart," Alec told her. "That's good enough for me."

"But not for me!"

He slid up the bed like a snake, his head between her legs, his palms spreading her glistening thighs. "Have you forgotten?"

Her heart raced. "Forgotten what, Alec?"

"How good I am at this."

That's all he said before diving in like an animal devouring its prey.

And, God, was she ready for him.

She squirmed as he wrapped his lips around hers, but he grabbed her hips and held her steady, right where he wanted her. She told her legs to kick him away, told her hands to swat at him, but her body wouldn't obey.

Her body wanted his mouth.

God, did her body want his mouth...

He started slow, melding the pressure of his tongue with the wet heat of her slick lips. He could always pinpoint her clit, right on target. How did he do that? It made her weak. She melted for him as he lifted her butt off the bed and held it aloft to eat her at a better angle.

She felt wide open for him. Fully visible. He knew her so well. Even after all the time they'd been apart he knew just how to lick her to make her writhe, and he kept doing it again and again. Her limbs felt even weaker now than before, but she didn't fight him. She let him devour her, sucking now, to alternate sensation. The licks made her groan, but when he sucked her entire mound, that's when she shrieked.

"You shouldn't be doing this," she said as her fingers found the strength to weave into his full head of hair. "Please, Alec. Don't make me come."

When he licked her clit in a fast striking motion, her legs found the power to wrap themselves around his back. Suddenly she was shoving her pussy in his face and he was moaning like he loved it. He sucked hard, making her swell and distend inside his mouth. She screamed his name and he reached up to stop her from bouncing.

Wrong. He reached up to grab her breasts. And squeeze. To pinch her pinky-peach nipples. Oh God, why did he have to be so good at this? If Alec were terrible in bed, it would be so much easier to ask him to stop this, stop it now.

But how can you tell a man to stop when you're on the verge of one of the most powerful orgasms of your life?

Tessa's thighs became a noose around Alec's neck, but he didn't seem to care. He just kept mashing his mouth against her mound, moving his head side to side, moaning even louder than she was—and Tessa was no timid kitten in bed! She could make noise with the best of them.

Would anybody hear?

She'd heard other voices when she'd opened the door, but no one had come to her rescue when she'd screamed for help before.

This time, she hoped to hell no one would come running. She didn't want this feeling to end.

Her thighs quivered against his neck. If he hadn't put on so much muscle mass since they were a couple, she'd have worried about snapping his head off his shoulders. She just couldn't help herself. His tongue pleased her so fully that she bounced on the bed, feeding him more of herself until she couldn't handle the sensation any longer.

She quivered and writhed. She bucked off the bed, but he pressed her down—both big hands on her swollen breasts. God, his skin was hot. Blazing hot. She could barely breathe around him, and the screaming made her throat run dry.

Alec backed off, perhaps sensing that she couldn't take any more. When he hopped off the end of the bed, she got a good look at the true extent of his arousal. Wow, was he ever turned on! He must really love eating her pussy.

"You need water," he said, and strode to the table to collect the bottle Denise had brought.

When he stood beside the bed, she arched up, propping her head on the pillows. Her hand wandered toward his dick, innocent as can be. Her fingers wrapped around that impressive girth. If she thought his hands were hot, they had nothing on his cock. It blazed in her hand, pumping out clear jets of pre-cum as she squeezed his shaft.

"Good to see the strength has come back to your extremities." He ran one hand through her hair, then forced her head back so he could pour a drizzle of water down her throat. It was practically pornographic, the way he hydrated her. Even when she'd had enough, he kept pouring. Water streamed out the side of mouth, spilling down her chest.

She laughed, and said, "Alec, you're getting me all wet."

He poured more clear, cool water between her breasts and it slid down her belly, then between her legs. "I thought you wanted a shower."

"A shower in the shower, not on the bed."

He winked. "How about a golden shower?"

She roared with laughter, slapping his dick, then pushing on his abs. Not that it made a difference. His stomach was hard as a rock.

"Did you just smack my cock, young lady?"

She faked being scandalized. "I would never do a thing like that!"

"Like hell you wouldn't." He went for his pants and took two things from his pockets: his keys and her phone.

When he sat next to her on the bed, she sighed. "You're going to tell me it's time to call off the wedding."

"Nope," he said. "That's already done."

11

When he showed her the text message, she really was scandalized. Sure he'd texted Sandra on her behalf, but this was something altogether different. Tessa was not the kind of girl who broke up with her fiancé by text.

The text Alec had written was surprisingly endearing, but that didn't stem the anger rising up in her belly. Tears welled in her eyes, and she blinked them back. She didn't want to show any signs of weakness when she said, "How could you do this to me?"

"Do what?" Alec asked. "Save your life?"

"You made me look like the kind of jerk who breaks up with someone by text!"

She swiped for her phone, but Alec held it away. She tried again, but he stood with the phone above his head.

Tessa didn't want to be the kind of girl who jumps up and down and squeals, "Give it back! It's mine!" Memories of the playground. Instead, she found herself battering Alec's chest with her closed fists. Not that it made the slightest difference. She obviously wasn't doing any damage. In fact, if his dick was any indication, he actually enjoyed her helpless attack.

"This isn't funny, Alec! Sean doesn't deserve to be treated this way."

"Yes he does," Alec boomed, and the intensity in his voice shocked her into submission. "Didn't you hear a word Denise said? Weren't you listening?"

"If I wasn't listening, I wouldn't have agreed to call off the wedding. But you should have let me do it face to face."

"Listen to me, Tessa." He took her chin in his hand and held it so hard she was forced to look at him. "Face to face he would have killed you. That really hasn't sunk in yet, has it?"

"It has," she said, pleadingly, but she knew he was right. She believed Denise. Intellectually, she felt the threat was real. But in her heart? Well, her heart was still stuck on him. Stupidly, maybe, but hearts were rarely sensible.

"I didn't want to have to do this," Alec said.

Tessa's heart trembled. Her stomach quaked, but her thighs... God, why was this turning her on? What was wrong with her?

"Do what?" she asked.

He looked at her phone and cleared his throat like he was about to recite a poem. Then he started reading Sean's responses. They started out baffled, which was understandable. She hadn't shown any signs that this was about to happen.

Alec had sent one text in response, simply to say, "I'm truly sorry."

"Sorry doesn't pay for a wedding. Do you know how much money I've spent on you?" He asked for the jewellery back, which was understandable, to Tessa. In fact, she found Sean's anger sweet, in a way. If he was this upset about losing her, he must love her a whole damn lot.

Maybe this was all a mistake. There was still time. She could marry him after all, if she could just escape from Alec.

"You're not convinced," Alec said.

He always could read her like a book.

"Okay," he said. "Fine. Then it's time for the voicemails."

Maybe it was Alec's intonation that coloured those texts a rosy shade, because when she heard Sean's actual voice, her stomach knotted. Tessa had never believed in the devil, but her worldview changed in that moment. The deep, icy anger in Sean's voice proved it without a doubt: he was evil incarnate.

All the time they were together, that's what was living beneath the surface? This calm, collected voice that was so cold, dead inside, making the most insidious threats she'd ever heard. "You think you can walk out on me? Oh no, baby. There is no escape. Wherever you go, I'm there. I've got eyes all over this city. You leave the city? I've got eyes all over the country. I've got eyes everywhere. You can't make a move that I won't know about. And when I find that pretty face? It won't be pretty for long."

Tessa ran for the toilet and dry-heaved into that stinking bowl. She wanted to excise her life with that man, eject it from her body. It hadn't sunk in until now what a terror Sean truly was.

Alec joined her in the bathroom and held her hair while she heaved, twisting it behind her head until it formed a knot.

"I guess you were right," she said.

"I'm sorry, Tessa. I really am." He handed her a pack of gum and she chewed three pieces. "I want the best for you. It's what you deserve."

She looked up at him, feeling like her insides had all spilled from her body, like she was wearing her organs on the outside.

He still looked at her like she was beautiful, even if she felt like a ghost of her former self.

"Do you trust me, Tessa?"

She nodded. Didn't even have to think about that one.

"So when I say the safest place for you is here with me, do you believe it?"

She did. But she had to ask, "Where are we?"

"It's better that you don't know."

"Why?"

"For the safety of everyone within these walls."

She remembered the laughter she'd heard in that dark hallway, and asked, "What's out there?"

He offered his hand and she took it, letting him lead her across the scuzzy motel carpet to the door with all the locks. When he brought her into the darkness beyond, she stayed so close behind him her breasts pressed against his back. She tried to ignore the searing sensation of his hot skin on her cold nipples, but it was impossible.

It felt strangely freeing to be naked in the total blackness of the hallway. She could feel carpet underfoot and could sense the walls at her sides, but apart from that it was just them in all their unseen nudity.

She reached for Alec's hand and instead found something more interesting. His erection had waned while he'd played Sean's voicemails—which was probably a good sign—but when she wrapped her fingers around it, it quickly returned to life.

Alec's breathing changed, and she half expected him to say, "Cut it out, Tessa!"

That's what the old Alec would have done.

The new and improved Alec pushed her against the wall with the entire mass of his body. She felt slick, glossy wallpaper against her backside as he moved his cock inside her fist.

"Spit out your gum," he said, and before the words were even out she felt his finger in her mouth, fishing for it. When he found the minty wad, he stole it away and mashed it against the wall beside them.

He kissed her, and memories came flooding to mind like the juices between her legs.

12

Alec always was good with his mouth, but he'd been reticent to show affection in public when they were a couple. Just look at them now! Absolute darkness. She didn't even know where she was, and he was kissing her hard and fast, sliding his dick from her hand and slipping it into the wetness between her legs.

When he pressed inside her, she gasped. Had his cock always felt so big? Or was it bigger in the dark?

She wanted to tell him how good it felt, but he wouldn't release her tongue from his mouth. And even if he did, she was so turned on she probably couldn't form words.

He wrapped his arms around her ass and lifted her off her feet, sliding her back up the wall. He'd never been this strong when they were a couple. Now his cock surged inside her while she ran her hands across his muscular shoulders. She wanted to touch every piece of skin, feel his heat on her palms.

Alec was still holding his keys and phone in one hand, and she could feel them pressing into her thigh as he ploughed her repeatedly. She leaned into his kiss so her head wouldn't bang against the wall. Could anybody hear them moaning into each other's mouths? Who else was here?

She touched his cheeks, feeling the sharp prick of whiskers. Her whole body responded. She wrapped her legs tighter around his waist and let him fuck her furiously against the wall. He was everywhere. Inside her and all around her. She wanted this forever. The friction was frenzied. He felt huge and she loved it, loved the motion, loved his exertion, loved every hitch and squeeze.

Tearing away from his kiss, she cried, "Yes, Alec! Yes!"

He covered her mouth with his palm, but his hand was so big it covered her nose as well, making it hard for her to breathe, let alone scream.

She whimpered into his hand. "Yes, Alec! God, yes!"

He dropped her to the floor, spun her around and pressed her breasts against the wall. He didn't remove his hand, but he did slide it down a touch so she could finally breathe.

Wrapping one arm around her waist, he fucked her furiously from behind. She savoured the sense of his front slapping her ass and his balls smacking her thighs. She tried not to scream, and keeping those feelings inside filled her with a heady mix of arousal and anxiety.

She wanted to let it all out. Her pussy clung to his dick as he pumped fast inside her. Her body reacted by milking him powerfully. She wanted to say to him: "See? I have strong muscles too. They're just on the inside."

But she couldn't say a word with his hand covering her mouth. She could only whimper like a puppy and give herself over to his lust.

He heaved his body inside hers, forcing her against the wall so hard she worried she'd go through it, end up in someone else's dank motel room.

Who else was here? What was this place?

He drove into her harder, faster, releasing her mouth in favour of her breast. When he squeezed it, her knees weakened, but he held her aloft, fucking her so hard she almost wondered if he'd switched places with some other man. Alec had always been an effective lover, in a kind and sensitive sort of way, but sex like this was unheard of.

And she loved it.

He drove her harder and faster against the wall, building her arousal, stirring her insides until her desire formed a tight knot ready to explode.

When it did explode, he came with her. His front to her back, pressing her breasts against the wall, he groaned into her ear as he squeezed her fleshy tits.

Every muscle in her body tightened, and when they relaxed again, she couldn't keep herself upright. Alec caught her as she fell into his arms, and laughed though they were both panting with exertion. "I know how you feel. What have you done to me?"

"What have I done to you?" she said with a laugh. "I'm not the one who kidnapped a bride two days before her wedding."

Lifting her over his shoulder, he carried her slowly down the dark hall. When he arrived at the door he wanted, he unlocked it and carried her over the threshold.

She was expecting just another motel room. What she got was 5-star accommodations.

"What is this place?" she asked when he'd set her down on a sleek white couch. She stood up from it, because the last thing she wanted to do was stain his nice furniture with sex.

He said, "This is home for the foreseeable future."

"You live here?" she asked.

"You do," he said. Then corrected that to: "We do."

Chandeliers. Chic grey tones. Luxury furnishings and contemporary patterns. It was nicer than anywhere she'd ever lived. Nicer than Sean's place, and that was saying something!

"These first few months are the most dangerous," he warned her. "Sean'll try to track you down, and if he finds you, you know what he'll do."

Tessa nodded, and she suddenly felt embarrassed by her nudity.

"Sorry," Alec said. "You must be cold. Come with me."

He led her to a beautiful bedroom and opened an amazing closet full of gorgeous new clothes.

"Whose are those?" Tessa asked.

"They're yours. I couldn't ask you to leave your old life behind and not replace it with something new."

She threw herself into the closet, trying on everything from dresses to comfy clothing. She was so excited about the new apparel she almost missed it when Alec said, "I've run it by your boss. You can work remotely. I wouldn't ask you to give up your job. You'll need that consistency to keep your mind occupied. Otherwise you might start questioning whether Sean was really that bad."

"Wait," Tessa said defiantly. "What did you tell my boss?"

"That it was medically necessary for you to work from home. I said I was your doctor."

Wearing a summer dress over pyjama pants, Tessa sat heavily on the bed. This was a lot to take in all at once. She asked, "Can Sandra come visit?"

He took a meaningful breath, then said, "We'll see about that. Not just yet."

"Oh."

"It's not safe for you to know where we are, so I'd have to bring her in secret."

"Why isn't it safe? You don't trust me?"

"No," he said gravely. "And you shouldn't trust yourself. Not yet. Because there will come a point where you'll question why you're here. You'll want to go back to Sean. That's why there are locks on the doors leading outside. No one gets in or our without my key or Denise's."

"There are other people here?"

"Other women like you."

"Held captive?"

"For their own good. For *your* own good."

"But who are you to make that decision?"

"If you saw a woman about to step in front of a speeding train, wouldn't you grab her and hold her back and not let go?"

"Yeah, but that's..."

"It's the same thing, Tessa. Sean is a speeding train and he's coming straight at you. And when he strikes, you will die a slow and painful death from the inside out. Your days will be unending fear. It's the same with every woman here."

Tessa wasn't sure how she felt about Alec taking control over other people's lives. She wanted to know what these other woman thought. "Can I meet them?"

"Yes." A slight blush crossed his cheeks and Alec said, "They're anxious to meet the one woman I could ever love. A lot of them have crushes on me, but I always say: I only have eyes for Tessa."

His affection was boyish and heartfelt, but his loving was masterful enough that she could still feel him inside her, even now.

Luxury accommodations. Locked in. New clothes. New everything. Cut off from the world, but living in a new world where everyone shared an experience most people would probably shame them for.

If you fall for a man who turns out to be evil, what does it say about you?

Tessa peeled the dress over her head and pushed down her pyjama pants. Naked on the bed, she let her guard down entirely. With Alec by her side, she let herself cry the tears of painful loss.

Her life would never be what she thought it would be. But at least she had him. At least she had this. Her new life: a fate much better than death.

Spite Sex

I still feel bad about this. I shouldn't have done it, no matter how angry I was. There's no excuse for cheating, but there are *reasons*. And here's mine.

Vicky and I were prone to the same kinds of arguments as straight couples, but when our hormones peaked, man oh man, we could tear a strip off one another. One Friday, we had a blow-out about nothing in particular. Vicky left my apartment, screaming, "Fuck you! Forget about your stupid concert!"

She was supposed to come to a little club downtown the next night, to watch a band I loved and she hated. When she said she wasn't coming, I believed her. Vicky was furious.

It just so happened that, two weeks before that argument, I'd received a pleading email from my ex-girlfriend. I broke up with Roma because she was way too intense for me, but she never gave up. She knew I was dating Vicky, but she didn't care. Roma didn't care about anyone but herself. I loved and hated her for that.

So, when Vicky and I had that huge fight, I thought, 'Fuck it! I'll invite Roma to the damn concert.' Maybe I needed to assert my independence, but more likely I just wanted to lash out. Vicky had said some really hurtful things, and I could never match her on name-calling.

But I could fuck someone else. There was no better revenge than spite sex.

The minute I spotted Roma outside that hole-in-the-wall tavern, my pussy pulsed—a thick throb, fast as my heartbeat. As I walked up to her, I could imagine the look on Vicky's face when I confessed to this. I couldn't wait to break her heart.

Roma grabbed me and I let her. We showed our tickets at the door, but my band wasn't up for another half-hour. As we crunched over peanut shells, Roma slid her lips across my cheek. I reminded her that I had a girlfriend. She said, "I don't care, and neither do you."

She was right. I asked her where, but that was a stupid question. She pulled me past the bar, and I followed like a dog on a short leash. My nipples were hard beneath my bra. I couldn't wait to feel her lips around them. Roma was such a great fuck, so passionate. I wanted her to take me.

Roma pulled me into the women's washroom, which was dingy as hell and only had two stalls. She kicked open the one that wasn't occupied, and slammed me inside, against the cold concrete wall. I could hardly breathe when she forced her lips against mine. I whimpered, but I didn't fight. After all, I wanted this.

The toilet in the next stall flushed, and I felt like such a slut, kissing my ex in a bathroom while some girl pissed next door. Roma grabbed at my corduroys, and when she couldn't get the fly undone fast enough, she ripped it open. I wasn't wearing any panties. Her hand found my heat quick as one-two-three. She attacked my pussy, shoving two fingers in my snatch and drawing my juice up, slathering it over my clit.

She was all over me, clutching my arm with one hand while the other smacked my clit. She spanked my cunt, slapped it. That thick pulse in my pussy had grown into something explosive.

Roma mashed her palm against me, and I screamed into her mouth. I couldn't even tell if there were other women in the bathroom, listening. When Roma rubbed my pussy hard and fast, I went wild, bucking like crazy, rubbing my wet cunt against her palm.

I don't know how she made me come so fast. I must have really wanted it, and the idea of hurting Vicky was so horribly appealing that I just wanted more, more, more.

Pushing down on Roma's shoulders, I begged her to lick my snatch. I didn't need to ask twice. She dropped to her knees on that dirty bathroom floor and spread my pussy lips with her thumbs. It didn't matter that I'd just come. I could do it again. I could come a thousand times over, given the inspiration. And Roma was damn good at providing inspiration.

She didn't lick my clit. No. She shoved her fingers up my snatch, and then she sucked. This was my favourite of her moves—that come-hither motion she made against my G-spot while she sucked mercilessly at my fat little bud. I thrashed against the concrete wall and groaned as I rubbed my cunt against her face, spreading pussy juice all around her lips and down her chin.

When I told her I was going to come again, she only worked harder. She fucked me with her fingers and sucked me with her mouth. She went wild between my legs until I was hollering, cursing—I couldn't control myself.

I couldn't remember the last time I'd come so hard, and all I could see were my girlfriend's tears. I wanted her to cry when I told her about this. It would hurt her, right to the core.

I let Roma suck my clit until I couldn't stand the pleasure. Her hunger still wasn't satisfied, apparently. She rose to her feet and kissed me, fondling my breasts over my top until someone started pounding on the door, saying, "I have to pee, you stupid dykes!"

Roma strutted out of the stall. I slunk behind her, tying my hoodie around my waist to cover the rip in my pants.

When we left the bathroom, my band was just setting up. I couldn't wait to get some booze down my throat. Roma went to order at the bar, and the minute she stepped away, that's when I saw Vicky.

I could tell by the look on her face that she was sorry. I'd forgiven her a million times before, just like she'd forgiven me. When my eyes met hers I knew I couldn't fuck this relationship up. I ran to the door and wrapped my arms around her, pulling her outside, away from Roma.

Vicky was confused. She kept saying, "What about your band?" but staying for the concert was just asking for trouble. I'd used Roma to get back at Vicky, but all I could do was run away.

I never answered Roma's emails after that, and I never told Vicky what happened. Cheating out of spite is inexcusable. That's why I can't come clean.

All the same, every time I think about that dirty bathroom sex with Roma, I get a little thrill. It might have been wrong, but it felt damn good.

Running in Circles

I always thought I was a little different from other women.

When most girls break up with their boyfriends, they seem to miss the kisses and cuddles, the uninhibited couple sex, and even just that extra body heat warming the bed. I don't know what was wrong with me. When I broke up with Lawrence, what I missed most of all was the delicious sensation of his hard cock against the softness of my mouth. That rigid but tender meat against my lips, against my tongue...

Merde, do I ever love giving head...

For years, there had been this attraction-repulsion thing going on between Lawrence and I. It's not that I was attracted to him and he was repulsed by me or vice-versa. No, the sentiment was mutual. We both loved and despised one another. Eventually, the love began to dwindle while the annoyances were in constant crescendo. We had broken up, and this time it was final. He broke a promise that meant the world to me. I never did get over it.

I'd been a hopeless back-slider in the past, but I was committed to making this break-up work. *Cosmo* instructed me to wash my sex sheets, pillow cases and anything else that might smell like my ex the minute he was out the door. His clothes went to Goodwill. *Good riddance!* What surprised me most was that I didn't cry at all this time around. I wasn't

89

thinking about him constantly. That's how I knew it was finally over between us. He wasn't dwelling on my mind.

When September rolled around and it was again time for the Terry Fox run for cancer research, I didn't think twice about going. Lawrence and I had run—ok, walk-jogged—the route for years. In fact, that's where we met. During the opening speeches, when survivors talked about their fights against cancer, I noticed a beautiful bald man in the crowd, wiping tears from his eyes with the sleeve of his T-shirt. There was nothing more moving to me than a man who could cry. I offered him a tissue. It was love at first wipe.

This year I invited our office manager Hildie to run with me. Sure she was pushing sixty, but so was Lawrence. Plus, Hildie hit the gym six days a week. I would be eating her dust. We'd asked our boss Herman to come along too, but he decided volunteering to roast wieners at the event was more his style. I just didn't want to go alone. Lawrence would be there. He always ran the Summerside route, arriving at eight-thirty on the dot to listen to the speakers. Out of some perverse desire to see how he was holding up without me, I asked the eternally-late Hildie to meet me at the same time.

Standing on the hill overlooking the crowd, I searched out my ex. He had to be there somewhere. *Yes, there he was!* Over by the parcel-check desk, in the blue wind-breaker and faded grey baseball cap. Lawrence was ripping off his tear-away pants to reveal black shorts and the athletic legs of a seasoned marathon runner. I thought my heart would explode. *Shit de merde*, those thighs still made me weak in the knees. As much as I hoped he wouldn't see me, his gravity began pulling me in. Suddenly I was walking toward him, without really wanting to. *No! Stop it, legs. Halt!* They weren't listening. They were propelling me into his gravitational field.

Hungarian dance, the disco version. My cell phone was ringing.

"Audrey? It's Hildie. I'm next to the registration booth, waving my hand in the air. Do you see me, girl?"

I did see her, after a while. In fact, Hildie was only a few feet away from me. To find someone in a crowd, one must really *want* to see them. Or really *not* want to. I could pick my ex out of a lineup by his baseball cap alone. He was over by the stage, listening to a twenty-three-year-old woman's story about her battle with osteogenic sarcoma. She'd been very fortunate not to loose her leg to cancer like Terry Fox did. "We've come a long way thanks to your generous support," she told the crowd.

Hildie lost her son Kofi to leukemia years before we started working together. After that, she became everyone's mother, including mine. Every time I broke up with Lawrence, hers was the shoulder I cried on. Had I given any indication that I was tempted once again by the *emmerdeur*, she would have clocked me one. *No way, Jose. I'm not cleaning up that mess again!* If I gave her any indication that my ex was at the run, Hildie would have thrown her water bottle at his head. She was so protective.

When the starter's pistol popped, we were off. Hildie and I passed Lawrence in the first minute of the run. Even just the sight of his bare calves had my body slobbering for him. I wished I could pause to take in the soapy fresh scent of his skin. *How did that man always manage to do this to me?* He could turn me on without even knowing I was there. One look at him and I was ready to pull him into the woods and fuck his brains out.

We hadn't yet reached the one kilometre mark when my side started cramping, but Hildie wouldn't let me slow her down. She had a time to beat. Thank God she let me drop back. There was no way I could have sprinted alongside that woman for ten Ks. And she nearly twice my age! I tried not to dwell on that too much.

A crowd of runners passed me by as I slowed my pace, glancing over my shoulder. Lawrence jogged up the woodland path. It was the perfect place for an ambush. The heavily treed area adjacent to the run route dropped off where a valley cut through the forest. When Lawrence passed me to the left, I tackled the bald beauty, sending him tumbling into the woods. We had a rough landing against the leafy forest floor, just far enough beyond the trees for no one to come investigating.

"What the..." he started. You should have seen the look on his face! Like a deer in the headlights, his blue eyes were startled wide open. I had to laugh.

"Audrey, where did...how did...what did you do that for?" he stammered, brushing the dirt from his *Marathon of Hope* T-shirt.

"I saw you taking off your pants before the run and I just wanted to tear off your shorts and suck you dry," I admitted, running my fingers against his solid thigh.

Lawrence's eyes glazed over and his meat jumped in his shorts. See, that was one of the many things I always loved about giving head—the very mention of the act could make a man hard.

As I slid down the leafy hill, the scent of musty earth rose up under my feet. From the foot of the treed dale, I stared up at my ex, from the bulge in his shorts to the gleam in his eyes. "What are you waiting for?"

He glanced over his shoulder at the race we were supposed to be running. "Someone might see us," he objected.

"No one will see us. There are too many trees in the way, and then there's the hill. Just get down here!" I was getting a tad impatient. It had been so many months, but the minutes were killing me. Just as I started to think I'd have to drag him down the hill, I noticed a change in his demeanour.

"Hey, let's go over there," Lawrence said, sliding down the knoll. He was pointing to a grouping of trees draped in late-season morning glories. Scurrying over, we found ourselves suddenly far from the crowds, the runners, from civilization as a whole.

Lawrence started to say, "I think we should talk about..." but I interrupted him with a hot, lingering kiss. Talking was the last thing on my mind, and Lawrence's penchant for small talk always did drive me nuts. *How's your brother? How's work? Did Herman get his promotion?* Blah, blah, blah! I would rather feel the undulations of his warm tongue against mine than hear it flapping on about nonsense. *Merde*, was he ever a good kisser! I'd already forgotten. His tongue seemed psychic, it was so responsive.

We tumbled to the forest floor, landing on the trunk of a fallen tree. With a sparkling sensation warming my cunt, I straddled my ex. Through our clothes, his hard cock pressed against my clit. Always after my ass, Lawrence slid his hands beneath my yoga pants and squeezed my cheeks. A growl rumbled from his throat and pulsed in my mouth as we kissed.

But dry humping my ex on a fallen log just wasn't going to cut it. I had to get that big warm cock in my mouth.

I sank to the ground. Maple leaves crunched under my knees.

"We said we weren't going to do this anymore," he whined.

Why was he always talking? Pulling on the waistbands of his black shorts and his underwear, I grabbed hold of Lawrence's familiar cock. Long and strong, just like I remembered.

"You said you never wanted to see me again..." he went on.

I didn't want to see him again. When I saw him, my skin turned to flames and I did things I shouldn't have done. For instance, I fellated him in the forest.

Lawrence's cock leapt at me the way a friendly Labrador jumps at a familiar face. He must have recognized me. *Well, I was always good to him. Took him out to play, gave him treats...*

With the back of my tongue, I issued gentle taps along the crease of his tip. Lawrence snorted like a baby pig. I always loved that sound. It meant I was doing something so good he couldn't control his ejaculations. Vocal ejaculations, of course. The softness of his tip against my tongue sent reams of warm pleasure pulsing through my core. It was softer than anything. Softer even than my lips, which I ran side to side against his pearl of precum.

I kissed that tender flesh, pressing down on it and sticking the tip of my tongue into the small groove of his tip. Lawrence couldn't help being turned on by my efforts. I loved that. The man was enfeebled by my mouth. That kind of control over him was the ultimate turn-on.

Gripping his cock by the base, I let my tongue swim circles around the tip. Lawrence whimpered. That helpless sound made my pussy clench. With his tender skin between my lips, I sank down on his rock-hard meat. His smoother than smooth tip hopped against my tongue. Slow motion was the key. I took a little bit more of his cock into my mouth, then slowly retracted. One step forward and two steps back. My tongue casually pulsed against his warm shaft. I loved that sensation. Nothing could be better than a familiar cock in my mouth, with its manly sex taste, the shaft hard on the inside and soft on the outside...how could it be both hard and soft at once? It was the best feeling in the world.

Again he whimpered when I wisped my fingertips along his inner thigh. Lawrence always did love those butterfly-wing sensations. When he took my head in his hands, I knew he wanted me to suck. *Merde*, I wanted to eat his meat, but I waited. If he wanted it so badly, he would have to ask. Lawrence never was much good at making requests, even though he knew I got off on hearing him beg. Dirty words were such a turn-on.

So, fully aware that Lawrence sought suction, I didn't give it to him. I wanted him to ask for it. Reaching into his double layer of shorts, I cupped his balls in my hand. While I nuzzled the squishy orbs, Lawrence scooched forward, pulling down his waistband to give me room to play. I dove at his balls, licking and flicking them, taking one then the other tickly sphere in my mouth. *Gently, gently.* He was far enough forward that I could send a finger down the path to his asshole. He gasped. *Oh, Audrey...*

He wanted me to suck him so badly, but I just licked the length of his shaft, waiting to be asked. "Audrey..." When I flicked the border between shaft and tip with my tongue, he yelped like a puppy. "Could you..." *Could I what?* I licked his shaft again, base to tip. "Could you please suck my cock?"

Bingo!

I GLANCED UP INTO LAWRENCE'S face. His sky blue eyes were pleading with me. That was the look I always got off on when I was younger. *He needed me.* With one hand grasping his shaft and the other cupping his balls, I took his rigid meat in my mouth. Lawrence roared like a bear just out of hibernation. That was the sound I'd been waiting to hear. Pumping his shaft and fingering his hole, I clamped the silken walls of my mouth around Lawrence's drooling cock. I worked my tongue around his straight-as-an-arrow rod. He let out sighs of pure relaxation, slipping into the warm bath of my mouth. The scent of cock hung heavy on the air, mingling with the musty odour of the forest floor in autumn. Just like kissing, but the tongue was hot and huge. At once, he was rigid and perfectly smooth.

Lawrence didn't thrust. He didn't do anything, just sat there gasping. This was the cock I dreamed of on sultry summer nights. I knew what it wanted and how it reacted. It couldn't think, it just responded. I licked it and it stiffened. I sucked it and it came. With a cock, there was no small talk, no dinner and a movie, and no complications. That stiff rod was more reliable than any man I'd met.

Through sharp breaths, Lawrence wheezed, "I'm afraid...I'm afraid...I'm afraid you might get a mouthful!"

Bring it on! I pumped harder and squeezed tighter. Above my hand, my head dove in syncopated rhythms, sucking that soft-hard flesh, that smooth-as-an-eyelid tip, until Lawrence cried out in pleasure-pain. My mouth became a black hole, devouring all of creation. I didn't feel him climax, though I'm certain he did because his body jumped, jumped, and jumped like his soul was escaping his flesh. A faint aftertaste of sweet vegetarian cum lingered on.

I couldn't have been more self-satisfied if I'd just won the Nobel Prize. When I nestled his spent cock back into its cloth house, Lawrence appeared dreamy and exhausted. I kissed his thigh, leaning my head on it to look into his face. *Were those crow's feet always there? Or had he aged that much over the past few months?* He was getting a little jowly too, or maybe it was just the angle.

"I knew it," he said, lost in bliss. "I knew you still loved me."

I breathed in sharply. The back of my throat burned and I rose abruptly to my feet. Maple leaves and dirt clung to my knees. I hit them off so roughly it hurt. "Who the hell said anything about love?" I scoffed. "I sucked your cock. Let's leave it at that. Shit, you always have to make things more complicated than they really are."

"But you wouldn't have done what you did if didn't love me," Lawrence said in that coy, childish tone that made my blood boil.

"When are you going to get it through your thick skull? It doesn't matter whether or not I love you. I might love you for the rest of my life, but that's not enough to keep us together."

"I'm so sorry," Lawrence pre-empted. He knew what was coming next.

"You *promised*, Lawrence. You promised me you were going to leave her and we would finally be together. I wanted us to be a real couple, not just some married guy and his mistress. Why would you promise me that when you knew you weren't going to follow through?"

"I'm sorry," he replied, staring down into the maple leaves. "I just wanted to make you happy."

"Lying to me doesn't make me happy!" I cried. "Broken promises don't make me happy! *Shit de merde*, Lawrence. What the fuck is wrong with you? Frickin' *emmerdeur*!"

I was out of words. Blinded by rage, my brain just spewed out French curses. I couldn't look at the miserable bastard any longer. My throat burned. I knew the tears were inevitable, but I didn't want to give him the satisfaction of seeing me cry.

Turning on my heels, I leapt up the leafy hill. It was slippery and I fell to my knees twice. My hands landed in mounds of dense soil and pushed me back to my feet. Pulling myself up by a line of thin birch trees, I launched myself back into the run for research. *Where was Hildie? I needed her again.* She was going to smack me, but when that was over she would hold me while I wept for everything I wanted and couldn't have. I picked up my pace, sprinting past the stragglers. If I ran fast enough, maybe I could elude the tears.

You might also enjoy:

The Other Side of Ruth
A Lesbian Novel
By Giselle Renarde

RUTH LOVES HER HUSBAND, but she keeps secrets from him. Big secrets.

When a notoriously lesbian neighbour returns home to Toronto from Art School in Montreal, Ruth finds herself unmistakeably attracted. Agnes is quirky, creative, and significantly younger. Despite their age difference, Agnes welcomes Ruth's attention.

But Agnes has secrets of her own. She plays hide-and-seek on Ruth, disappearing for months at a time. Where does she go? And what emotions are brewing between Ruth's husband and his closest friend? Everyone on the block seems to be hiding something, and Ruth isn't sure how long she can conceal her true self from the neighbours.

After twenty-five years married to a man, can Ruth find a place in her life for ambiguous, artsy Agnes? Or will the younger woman's demons devour them both?

Now Available as an ebook, audiobook, and in print!

ABOUT THE AUTHOR

Giselle Renarde is an award-winning queer Canadian writer. Nominated Toronto's Best Author in NOW Magazine's 2015 Readers' Choice Awards, her fiction has appeared in well over 100 short story anthologies, including prestigious collections like Best Lesbian Romance, Best Women's Erotica, and the Lambda Award-winning collection Take Me There, edited by Tristan Taormino. Giselle's juicy novels include Anonymous, Cherry, Seven Kisses, and The Other Side of Ruth.

Giselle Renarde
Canada just got hotter!
Want to stay up to date? Visit
http://donutsdesires.blogspot.com[1]!
Sign up for Giselle's newsletter: http://eepurl.com/R4b11
Weekly Audio Erotica at http://Patreon.com/AudioErotica

---

1. http://donutsdesires.blogspot.com/

2

Milton Keynes UK
Ingram Content Group UK Ltd.
UKHW020641080923
428296UK00013B/592